AN ARMY OF ELEVATED SEA ANIMALS!

Swaying above them, outlined against the fresh morning sky, were the ominous shapes of the whales. They towered thirty feet high, their eyes glowing. They had spread their flukes. They drooled from their wet baleen. They bared their teeth (those that had them).

Lily stopped on her bike and stood for a second at the crest of a hill. She stared with horror at the scene of destruction down in the valley before her.

The whales did whatever the radio tower commanded. They stepped on used car dealerships and a putt-putt golf course. They burned down trees in a trice with their laser-beam eyes. They stalked in rows through the countryside.

They had to be stopped.

WHALES ON STILTS

**RUN OUT AND BUY ABSOLUTELY
EVERY SINGLE ONE OF THE
OTHER TITLES WE'RE PUBLISHING
IN THIS THRILLING SERIES!**

The Clue of the Linoleum Lederhosen

WHIZZZZZZ

WHIZZZZZZ

M. T. Anderson's Thrilling Tales

WHALES
ON
STILTS

M. T. ANDERSON

Illustrations by **KURT CYRUS**

HARCOURT, INC.

ORLANDO   AUSTIN   NEW YORK
SAN DIEGO   TORONTO   LONDON

3

Requests for permission to make copies of any part of the work should
be submitted online at www.harcourt.com/contact or mailed to the following address: Permissions Department, Harcourt, Inc., 6277 Sea
Harbor Drive, Orlando, Florida 32887-6777.

www.HarcourtBooks.com

Cover illustration copyright © 2005 by Eric Bowman
Excerpt from *The Clue of the Linoleum Lederhosen*
copyright © 2006 by M. T. Anderson

First Harcourt paperback edition 2006

The Library of Congress has cataloged the hardcover edition as follows:
Anderson, M. T.
Whales on stilts/M. T. Anderson; illustrations by Kurt Cyrus.
p. cm.
Summary: Racing against the clock, shy middle-school student Lily
and her best friends, Katie and Jasper, must foil the plot of her father's
conniving boss to conquer the world using an army of whales.
[1. Best friends—Fiction. 2. Adventure and adventurers—Fiction.
3. Whales—Fiction. 4. Scientists—Fiction. 5. Science fiction.]
I. Cyrus, Kurt, ill. II. Title.
PZ7.A54395Wh 2005
[Fic]—dc22 2004017754
ISBN 978-0-15-205340-6
ISBN 978-0-15-205394-9 pb
ISBN 978-0-15-206212-5 SBF ed.

Text set in Stempel Garamond
Designed by Liz Demeter

A C E G H F D B

Printed in the United States of America

To my cousins
Ham and Santa
— M. T. A.

WHALES ON STILTS

CAREER DAY

On Career Day Lily visited her dad's work with him and discovered he worked for a mad scientist who wanted to rule the earth through destruction and desolation.

Up until then life hadn't been very interesting for Lily. There had not been very many mad scientists. She lived in a small town called Pelt. There was a supermarket and a library, and several minimalls with discount clothing outlets. The highway went through, and people were pulled over by the police if they drove more than five miles above the speed limit. It was that kind of town.

Most people didn't know that Lily herself was interesting. She watched things a lot, and thought about them a lot, but she didn't say much, except to her closest friends. She hid behind her bangs. When she needed to see something particularly important, she blew on her bangs diagonally upward, either from the left or the right side of her mouth. Her bangs parted like a curtain showing a nose-and-chin matinee.

Lily believed that the world was a wonderful and magical place. She believed that if you watched carefully enough, you could find miracles anywhere. The town's baseball team had a secret handshake that went back to the time of the settlers. A professor down the street had a skeleton hanging in his vestibule. Behind the dry cleaner, some ladies held newt races. There were interesting things like this everywhere, waiting to be noticed. Though Lily thought that she herself was too quiet and too boring to ever do anything interesting, she believed that if she just was watchful enough and silent enough—so silent that no one could even tell she existed—she would eventually see marvels.

Of course, she didn't expect that she would

see any marvels at her dad's work on Career Day. She didn't know what he did at his job, but it didn't sound unusually exciting or flabbergasting. She thought it would be nice to know what her father did—that way she could understand a little bit more of what her father and mother talked about at dinner—but she certainly didn't suspect that the visit to her dad's work would eventually lead to daring escapes, desperate schemes, brilliant disguises, and goons with handguns.

No, frankly, it would have been hard to figure that out, based on what she'd heard about her dad's work from little things he said. For example:

- "I'll stop and get those shirts from the cleaner. It's on the way home from work."
- "A guy at work had his wisdom teeth removed as an adult."
- "I spilled it on my pants at work."
- "I'm going to be home late from work."

There was not much that suggested hidden lairs. Terrifying invasions. High-tech weaponry. That also goes for statements like:

- "I spent the whole day at work circling number threes for the Dorsey account."
- "I'll take the day off work for the Annual Invertebrates Festival."
- "At work we could really do with some air-conditioning."

Or even:

- "The vending machines at work just got these little packages of muffins. Eighty-five cents. I could eat a whole package at once."

There really was not much to suggest that this would be a day unlike any other in Lily's life. When Lily got into her dad's car on the morning of Career Day, ready to hang out in his office, she was interested but not exactly expecting something thrilling.

Her dad drove for a while, eating cinnamon toast with one hand.

"I don't even know *where* you work," said Lily.

Her father gestured with his toast. "Edge of town," he said. "Abandoned warehouse."

"Abandoned?" she said.

"Yeah. Mmm-hmm." His mouth was full.

She asked, "What do you do?"

"Very complicated," he said. "Very."

The abandoned warehouse sat near the bay between a business called Nullco and a factory that made industrial filling. There were old chain-link fences around everything. Lily's dad parked in the lot. They got out and walked over to the abandoned warehouse. It was made of old bricks, and all the windows were black with soot and broken. There was a big spray-painted wooden sign that said:

ABanDIn WAREHOUSE.
STAY OUT!!!
THErE ARE PrOBly ScoRPiOnS!

Lily's dad lifted the sign and turned an old pipe that stuck out of the wall. A secret door slid open. He walked in.

Inside there was a desk with a receptionist. The receptionist said hello to Lily's dad and gave a big smile. "Good morning, Mr. Gefelty," she said.

"Good morning, Jill," he said. "How are things today?"

"I'm okay, I guess," said the receptionist. "Except I'm having pains in my knees from doing something stupid with a big round of cheese."

"I'm sorry to hear that, Jill," said Lily's dad.

He showed his badge, and the receptionist clicked a button that let them through a door.

They walked into a laboratory. People in lab coats were holding test tubes over flames. There were beakers and lasers and so on. Bunsen burners and alembics and computers. You know the drill. Everything looked incredibly top secret. Lily was blowing her bangs out of her face as quickly as she could. She glanced at everything they passed. She was amazed.

"What is this place?" said Lily. "Dad?"

Lily's dad looked bored. "Research and Development," he said.

She looked around again. He took her wrist and dragged her forward. "Come on, honey," he said. "They don't like people to look at what they're working on. After a minute the guards start shooting. First near your feet, then at your knees."

The guards stood with big guns next to all the doors, watching everything and frowning.

Lily rushed to catch up with her father. She grabbed at his sleeve. She whispered, "What do you make here?"

"I don't know," he said. "I'm in Sales and Marketing."

"Dad, you must know. There's something weird going on here."

"What's gotten into you?"

Careful to keep walking, she whispered,

"This is like some sort of mad scientist's laboratory. What do you really make here?"

"Oh," said her father, laughing. "A 'mad scientist's laboratory'? Nothing quite so sinister. I think your imagination has gotten the better of you. No, honey, it's all completely aboveboard. But it's kind of complicated to explain." He patted her arm. "Keep walking. The guards're looking antsy."

They reached a staircase and started up. Lily lingered behind, looking back at the lab.

"What's wrong?" her dad asked.

Lily blew the hair out of her face and looked straight at him.

"Oh, come on, honey," he said. "It's not really as suspicious as it seems. We're a midsize company devoted to expanding cetacean pedestrian opportunities."

She looked confused.

He smiled. "We make stilts for whales. See? Nothing suspicious."

"But ..."

Her father stuck his hands in his pockets and jogged up the steps, whistling. The tune was "How Much Is That Doggy in the Window?"

"Dad ...?" she protested, but her voice was too soft, and he was already a flight above her.

BREAK AND BRINE

Lily's dad's office was large and kind of bare. He had a desk and a computer and a phone. He sat her down in a chair over in one corner and read his e-mail. He drank some coffee. He typed some things.

Lily wanted to get up and explore the abandoned warehouse, but she knew she wouldn't be allowed. She had brought along some homework, but she couldn't really concentrate on it. Not while sitting in the middle of an extremely dangerous, highly guarded high-tech, secret scientific laboratory.

She tried to work on math. She told herself that there weren't really mad scientists, and that if there was a mad scientist, the worst place he or she could build a lair would be in an abandoned warehouse, because that's where everyone looked for mad scientists. But she kept on hearing weird beeping noises through the walls.

At about ten thirty, Lily's father took her down to the break room to get some of the little muffins that came in packages. She kept her eyes wide open to see what she could notice. She had always wanted to see what the break room in a mad scientist's laboratory looked like.

It was kind of like any other break room, with vending machines for candy, chips, and soda, and an old microwave, and some tables and chairs. The door of the microwave had been slightly melted by something hot.

"Hey there, Gefelty," said a man in a chair. "How're you doing?"

"I'm doing just fine, Ray," said Lily's father. "What's up?"

"Nothing much," said Ray, yawning. "Just the usual. We're a little bit behind schedule. But you know, sometimes it almost makes me curious—why all of the giant, destructive lasers? And why all of the maps of North America?"

"Yeah. Sure. I guess. Oh, Ray, have you seen the memo about the meeting with Paul?"

Ray looked both ways, like he was about to say something important.

Lily held her breath. She pretended to be interested in the candy selection.

Ray said quietly, "Okay. You know, it's only my opinion, but I think that Sandy should have been in charge of that project, not Paul. I mean, Paul's a great details person, but he doesn't always get the overall picture—you know what I mean? And Sandy's good both with details and with the big picture. But you know, Sandy doesn't get on so good with Loretta, and I think that's why they hired Paul after that whole thing with Bob and Sheila."

Mr. Gefelty said, "I agree, but—hey there, Larry!"

Both men straightened up when someone who was obviously the boss came in. The newcomer was dressed in a pin-striped suit, very natty, with a grain sack over his head with two holes cut out for his eyes.

"Hey, boys," he said. "Everything well?"

"Larry," said Mr. Gefelty, "I'd like you to meet my daughter, Lily."

Larry held out a blue, rubbery hand. "Hi, Lily. Nice to meet you."

Lily was shy, especially of blue, rubbery, concealed people, and so she didn't say much. She shook his hand.

"Say hi to Larry, Lily," said her father.

"Hi," said Lily. "It's very nice to meet you."

"She's a charmer, Gefelty. She'll sweep 'em right off their feet. Oh, hey, Gefelty, can I get that report from Sheila on my desk ASAP? I want to pass it on to R and D."

"Sure thing, Larry."

"Great. Great! Hey, the little girl reminds me—when are you planning to go on vacation with your beautiful family?"

"Oh, next month, once school's out."

"Oh, great, great. Where you planning on going?" asked Larry, opening the fridge, and pulling out a large vat of green brine and lifting it over his head.

"We're going to go visit Lily's grandmother in Decentville."

"You from there?" asked Larry.

"My wife."

"Oh, great, great," said Larry, dumping the vat of brine over his head so it soaked his grain sack and his suit. He put down the empty metal vat. "Oh, wait a second. Wait a second, Gefelty. Just thought of something. By then, I will have taken over the world, and Decentville, er, you know . . ." Larry made a noise that sounded like several large futuristic lasers blowing up the Decentville police station and the Bijou Theater and the rest of the town being engulfed in flames and destruction as car alarms went off in deserted burning alleyways.

Lily's father bit his lip. "Aw, shoot," he said. "Well, we'll reschedule."

"Best thing for it," agreed Larry, nodding his shrouded head. "Best thing." He clapped Lily's dad on the shoulder. "Oh, hey, hey—question for you: Do you guys prefer the nondairy creamer or real milk for the coffee?"

"Could the office stock both?" asked Ray.

"Well, see, the milk keeps going sour before it's used. That's what I'm worried about."

Ray nodded sadly. "That's what milk does," he said.

"You betcha; that's milk for you," said Larry. "I'm thinking of switching the office over entirely to the nondairy." He sighed, and they all thought about it for a minute. Then Larry said, "Awrighty. I'll see you guys later. Lily, it's nice to meet you. Have a great day at the office." He left the room with a wave, dripping brine.

"See?" whispered Ray. "This is what we have to put up with at this place."

Mr. Gefelty nodded. "You'd prefer the milk."

"Of course I'd prefer real milk! Who wouldn't? Huh? Tell me."

Lily's head was spinning. In just a few weeks her grandmother's town would be in flames and the mysterious Larry would be ruling the world! Lily felt like she couldn't move, couldn't breathe. Her dad just sipped his coffee. She steadied herself against a table.

On the wall was a poster of a kitten clinging to a branch. The caption said: "Just Hang in There! Kibble's on the Way!"

The cat, however, just looked terrified.

DESKSIDE ANXIETY

Lily and her father sat in his office.

This situation was too big for Lily. She didn't have the first idea of what to do.

She tried talking to her father.

"Dad...Don't you think that Larry is... strange? I mean...how he wants to take over the world?"

"Honey, sometimes adults use irony. They don't really mean what they say."

"He poured that...brine all over his head!"

"He has a skin condition, Ms. Nosy."

"But—" said Lily.

"Sweet pea, don't let your imagination go

crazy. We're just a cetacean prosthesis company in an abandoned warehouse."

"But, Dad—"

"Honey, do you see all the things on my desk? I have to do all these things." He picked up a piece of paper. "This thing, and..." (another piece of paper) "this thing and..." (stick-it note) "this thing..." (folder) "and even this thing. So why don't you do your homework and let me do what I have to do?"

So Lily quietly worried. She thought that Larry was pulling the wool over his employees' eyes. He was going to try to take over the world. She didn't know how, but she believed that was what he was after. What could she possibly do? She was just one person, just a *short* person— and Larry was an adult, a full-grown blue, rubbery, concealed adult, taking over the world. What could she possibly do? This thought filled

her

with

terror

like huge words filling a bleached pale-white page.

She decided she needed help.

Quickly.

KATIE AND JASPER

There was no question who Lily should ask for help: her two best friends, Katie and Jasper. Lily thought of herself as just a boring, quiet girl— but she knew she had interesting friends. Katie and Jasper had been through a lot of adventures, and were famous for their bravery and heroism.

Katie Mulligan lived in Horror Hollow, a little suburban development just off Route 666. Living in Horror Hollow, Katie had had lots of experience with zombies, werewolves, and flesh-eating viruses. She even had her own series of books about her adventures—the Horror Hollow series—and a fan club. If people sent $10.99, they got a monthly newsletter, a Horror Hollow Ghost Hunter's Kit, and a badge that had a picture of Katie screaming (from that time at the end of seventh grade when her blood had been taken over by a rogue mind-sloth and forced to flow backward).

Lily and Katie had been friends long before Katie became famous from her first book, *Horror Hollow #1: Entrée for the Beetle People*. Katie never even talked about her fan club, or how she was always being interviewed by writers for the series. Still, Lily knew that Katie was smart, quick, and brave—all things that Lily didn't think she herself was.

Lily's other friend was Jasper Dash, Boy Technonaut. Jasper enjoyed inventing things. He didn't mix with other kids much, probably because he dressed in gray wool shorts, long socks, a Norfolk jacket, and an aviator's cap. He had been on many adventures, and he'd also had a series of books written about him, including *Jasper Dash and His Amazing Electrical Sky Train* and *Jasper Dash and the Villainous Brain Pirates of Chungo*. Jasper had once had a fan club a few years back, sponsored by Gargletine Brand Patented Breakfast Drink. Kids who wrote to him and included a single thin dime got decoder rings and balsa-wood airplanes.

Recently, however, very few kids had been drinking Gargletine Brand Patented Breakfast Drink—it tasted awful and caused seizures in lab rats—so not many kids signed up for the Jasper Dash, Boy Technonaut, Fan Club. Jasper didn't seem to notice, though, because he was too busy whizzing around the skies in his inventions, making new appliances for his father, being gallant, solving the riddles of Creation, stunning crooks, and fighting off yeti in diamond mines.

You can see why, with friends like these, Lily might not think that she led the most adventurous life.

Both Katie and Jasper often told Lily that she was a hero just waiting to happen. They both admired her for many reasons. Lily herself didn't know what those reasons were. She was just happy that Katie and Jasper were her friends.

She felt sure that they would be able to get her out of her terrible predicament.

As soon as she got home from her father's work, Lily called them on the phone. She asked if there was someplace they could meet. She said it was really important. Jasper said they could come over to his place and have a cool sherbet smoothie in his airship snack bar, which had been featured in *Jasper Dash and His Astounding Aero-Bistro*.

The Aero-Bistro was a restaurant that floated above the town of Pelt. It was very beautiful in its design, with lots of wrought-iron fixtures and gigantic potted ferns everywhere. The air in the bistro was always warm, and the androids that served the customers all wore bow ties.

A professional ragtime band played just outside the windows, suspended in a helium gazebo.

The three friends sat at a table, and Lily told her story. Katie and Jasper looked very serious while they listened.

"I don't know what to do," Lily said.

"Maybe this Larry man was just being funny. But he didn't sound like it. I think something very bad is going to happen. And the worst thing is, my dad could be in danger!"

Katie said, "Hmm. Whoa."

Jasper said, "Dash it all, chums, this sounds a mighty pickle."

Yup, get used to it, because that's how Jasper always talked.

Lily said, "I thought you two would be able to help. Since you're . . . you know."

Jasper tapped his finger on his chin and looked up thoughtfully at the ceiling.

Katie said to Lily, "You know what I always do when I have a problem?" She sucked on her sherbet. "I always just ignore it for a few days. And after a few days—*voilà!* Guess what happens." She waved her sherbet spoon in the air. "Whatever I'm having a problem with? It decides it's going to break into my house and kill me, and so it breaks in and I run upstairs screaming, and just in the nick of time—blah blah blah

26

blah blah blah blah." She sat back in her chair and snorted. "Let me tell you: It's no way to live."

Jasper declared, "I think that infiltration may be our game." His blue eyes were thin and crafty. He held up one finger. "What we need to do is gather some information—and we need to gather it without anyone connecting us to your father and so endangering him. And I know just the thing that might do the trick."

"What's that?" said Lily.

"Lily," he said, "by gum, this is just the moment for a photocopier repairman."

Katie started laughing. Her spoon clanked in her sherbet smoothie. Then she stopped. "Oh," she said. "You weren't kidding?"

But no, he was not kidding. Jasper Dash had a plan.

Operation Xerox

About a week later Lily and Katie took a different bus than usual from school. They were going to get off the bus at the Abandoned Warehouse, where they would meet Jasper. Jasper wasn't with them because he didn't go to school. He had already received a PhD in Aegyptology.

Katie was looking at her gums in her reflection on the windows. She said, "Wouldn't it be weird if people had no lips? Only gums and teeth?" She looked at Lily. "Huh? What do you think? Would that be weirder, or if people had skis for feet?"

Lily didn't answer.

"What's wrong?" asked Katie. "You're not nervous, are you?"

"I'm a little nervous," admitted Lily in a whisper. "This is dangerous."

What is she talking about? Well, my friend, it's simple enough to tell: The previous week Jasper had gone into the Abandoned Warehouse dressed as a photocopy repairman. He had added a special secret addition to the photocopier. Whenever someone made a copy, his special secret addition made another copy and stored it for him.

Now all three of them were going to sneak into the building, disguised as other photocopy repairpeople, and they were going to see what photocopies had been made during the week. Then they would have a better sense of what Larry and his crew were *really* up to.

As you can see, this could be very dangerous.

It was even more dangerous, in fact, than Lily and her friends knew. Why?

I'll tell you.*

As Lily and Katie bumped along over

---

*Are you grateful? If so, I like carrot cake.

potholes toward the Abandoned Warehouse, Lily's father walked into the photocopy room and found his boss looking kind of strangely at the photocopier.

"Huh," said Larry. "Was this photocopier always this big?"

The photocopier took up most of the room. There were a huge number of brass pipes running all over the place, and lots of gears and cranks that turned. Sometimes valves would release steam. The whole room vibrated.

"Uh, no," said Mr. Gefelty over the racket. "The photocopy repair guy came in and added some stuff. You know—little guy, about twelve, thirteen years old? He added a lot of these new parts. For example, it didn't work by mule before."

Larry walked over to the mule's treadmill. "I knew I didn't recognize the mule. Is this a push-button mule?"

"No," said Mr. Gefelty. "That's a real kind of mule. That's a mule that you could ride to the

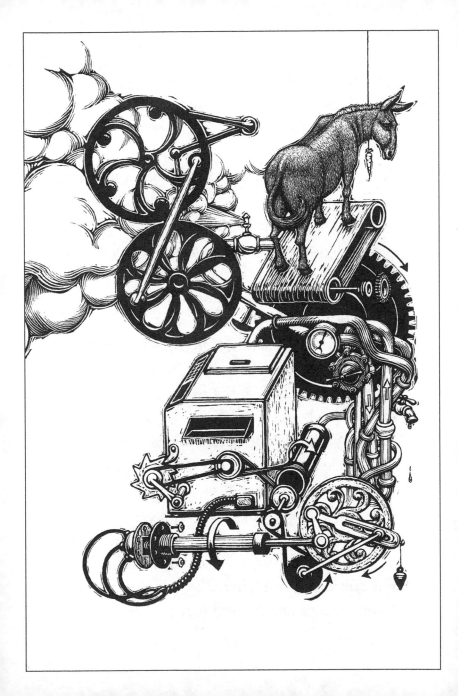

bottom of the Grand Canyon on, if you're real careful and balance your fishing rods."

"Gefelty?" said Larry. "I'm not sure about this. Grand Canyon aside, I'm starting to wonder if this isn't some kind of clever attempt at spying on our organization."

Gefelty shrugged. "Come on, Larry. Why would anyone want to spy on our organization? I mean, what do we do? Make stilts for whales. What could be wrong with that? Who could complain?"

"Yeah. Yeah. Thanks, Gefelty. Why don't you go back to your office? Don't come out for a while. Take a vacation, but in your office. I have some ideas about this. Will you excuse me?"

Larry squinted through his grain-sack hood. He walked away briskly to talk to his guards.

Meanwhile, back out on the streets of Pelt, Lily was getting anxious on the bus. She was a quiet girl, and not used to risk and danger.

Katie put her arm around Lily's shoulders and talked gently to her. She said reassuringly, "Don't worry about anything. Just concentrate on the plan. It'll be fine. We're going to have dinner at the Burger Meister until work lets out. Okay? Nothing difficult there. Eating. Chew the food, swallow. You've got that covered? Then we're going to go into the bathroom. Okay? And we're going to change into our photocopy-repair disguises. Okay so far? You've changed clothes before?" She bumped her friend with her elbow and smiled. Lily smiled back at her. Katie said, "So far so good? Then we're just going to walk down the street to the Abandoned Warehouse. You've walked down streets before? Just checking. And then, just when they're about to close down for the night, we're going to ask if we can go in to recall a part of the photocopier. Then we go in, take apart Jasper's whole special part of the photocopier, pick up the microfilm that has all the secret copies on it, and carry it all out past the armed guards while pretending we're like thirty-five-year-old professionals." Katie realized that the last part of the description didn't sound as easy as the first part.

She cleared her throat.

She and Lily looked at each other. Then they looked away from each other.

Katie cleared her throat again. Then she looked into the window at her gums. She said, "To change the subject, do you think I could tell if I had gingivitis?"

"Somehow this doesn't seem like a good idea," said Lily. "But probably that's just because I don't have any experience with this kind of thing. You know—adventure. Actually doing anything."

"Lily," said Katie, "would you stop that? You read about all kinds of amazing things. You have all sorts of amazing dreams. And you're the one who realized that this place was a mad scientist's headquarters in the first place!"

"We don't even know for sure if it is," Lily muttered. She hoped that she wasn't just leading them on a wild-goose chase.

Katie sighed and rolled her eyes. "Hello? Who else starts a small business in an abandoned warehouse?"

Lily leaned forward, resting her elbows on her knees. Her hair hid her eyes.

The bus rattled through the streets of Pelt and down to Smogascoggin Bay. It went past muffler repair stores and bagel bakeries. It went under a lot of phone lines. Finally, it reached the abandoned warehouse district. Lily and Katie picked up their backpacks and got off.

Jasper was there waiting. He was already in his photocopier repairman disguise. Unfortunately, Jasper was sort of out of touch and didn't really know what a photocopier repairman would look like, so he had just taken his best shot at it, which meant a sparkly brown jump-suit with big rings around his shoulders and elbows, and a helmet with an antenna and fins. He wore a utility belt with a screwdriver, wrenches, and a ray gun. There was a logo on his back that said: *Glorux Velp—Ace Photocopier Repairman—Venus Colony*.

"Jasper," said Katie, squeezing his padded shoulders, "it's good that we love you. Because otherwise, we'd never be seen with you any-where."

"I am cleverly disguised," he explained, "as the photocopier repairman of the future, when man, through his ingenuity, will conquer even the farthest reaches of space, and need to make duplicates of things."

Lily and Katie stared at him. He looked sheepishly down at his moon boots and said, "Look, chums, I got into the building wearing this last week."

Katie looked at her watch. "It's only three thirty," she said. "Let's go hang out for an hour or so before we come back to the warehouse and try to get in."

They walked down the street to the Burger Meister. The pavement was cracked. All around them were ruined mills and warehouses.

They sat at the Burger Meister for a while and ate fries. They talked about school and kids they knew.

Jasper began to notice that people in the

booths around them were snickering at his outfit. He tried not to take it personally. He forgave
them immediately. He figured they just needed
time to get used to the clothes of the future. He
held his head in various noble attitudes, as if
he were gazing up at three pink moons while
the sonic winds of X-terra blew across his chin.
Other kids kept pointing at him. Finally, he
took his helmet off and put it on his knees.

He crouched in toward the fries and tried to
be inconspicuous. That was made harder by his
glittery brown jumpsuit.

Katie and Lily were talking about the Abandoned Warehouse.

Lily was saying, "Officially, the company,
it's called Deltamax. I tried calling them on the
telephone the other day and asking what their
business was. Whoever answered their phone
just told me that it was very complicated."

"How long has your dad worked there?"
Katie asked.

"Two years." Lily sipped her soda. "I asked

him what he knew about his boss, Larry—the one who wears the sack over his head?"

"Yeah?" said Katie. "What'd he say?"

"He doesn't really know much. Larry never talks about his family or anything. Nobody knows where Larry's from, or anyplace else he's worked. No one knows how old he is."

"But has anybody even seen his face?" Katie asked.

"Nope," said Lily. "That's the thing. Nobody even knows what he looks like. He could be some famous master criminal, and nobody would even know it."

"Great Scott!" cried Jasper Dash, Boy Technonaut, slamming his fist down on the table. "Will these cads never cease mocking my jumpsuit?"

"Jasper," said Katie, "I think you're going to have to let this one go."

Jasper frowned deeply and fiddled with the ketchup.

Lily looked at her two friends. She felt proud

to be with them—especially because Jasper wasn't afraid to dress stupidly in public. Lily never wanted to have the kind of friends who refused to eat fries in a sparkly brown jumpsuit. She smiled, softly, under all of her hair.

Pretty soon it was time for Katie and Lily to put on their photocopy-repair uniforms, too. Katie was lending Lily a disguise. Katie's family, living in Horror Hollow, had a wide variety of weird disguises, because you never knew when you were going to need to pretend to be, for example, a census taker in an alien spacecraft while trying to get your little brother out of the meat locker.

Katie and Lily went into the women's room and changed their clothes. They stuffed their school clothes into their backpacks. When they came out, Jasper was flipping through the play-list cards on the jukebox, looking for the symphonic works of Sibelius.

"Heigh-ho, then," he said. "Off to work."

The three of them walked back down the

street, down the cracked pavement, to where the Abandoned Warehouse sat on the docks. It was almost five o'clock, and some of the employees were already slipping out of the secret door and going across the street to the Abandoned Parking Lot and getting into their cars. Lily had a mustache, so her father wouldn't recognize her. It was bushy and brown, and it tickled.

They opened up the secret door and stepped inside. There, in front of them, was Jill, the receptionist.

"Hello and welcome to Deltamax Industries, taking over the world through stealth and advanced laser technology since nineteen ninety-eight. How may I direct you today?"

"Ma'am," said Jasper, who was always very polite to his elders, "we're here to fix the photocopier. I came last week and installed some new elements that are apparently giving you trouble."

"Let me see if you have an appointment," Jill said, smiling and looking down at a clipboard.

"Oh—" said Katie. "We don't have an appointment, but we got a call that—"

"Yup, here you are!" said the receptionist, making a check mark. "You're expected. Please go right in. The photocopy room is through the secret laboratory, up two flights, and down the hall on your right."

The three of them looked at one another.

"What luck," said Jasper.

"'Luck,'" said Katie suspiciously, and exchanged a glance with Lily.

Lily scratched her mustache uncomfortably. She didn't like the look of this.

When they got upstairs, the girls were kind of surprised to see exactly how much machinery Jasper had added to the photocopier. The whole room was making a thrumming noise while all of the gears and cranks and pistons and the mule turned belts and made metal arms go up and down.

"Um, Jasper," said Lily, "this isn't really what we expected."

"Quick," whispered Katie. "Where are the microfilms?"

Jasper cocked his head. "Pardon?"

"The microfilms."

"Once more?"

"The microfilms."

"Yes. I see." He nodded. "So what are microfilms?"

"*Jasper!*" said Katie. "Your machine was supposed to be making duplicate copies of all of the things that were photocopied during the week!"

"Yes indeed. And so it did." He flung open a panel. "All ingeniously copied and transcribed onto one convenient wax roll, quite easily carried between the three of us." He hefted one end of the wax roll; it was as big as a carpet. "Come along. It's a mere two hundred and twenty pounds. Try to keep one hand free for making fists. We may have to bash our way out of here."

" 'May,' " said Larry. "Just *may*?"

"That was my assessment," said Jasper, kneeling in front of the machinery.

Suddenly he looked up. "Ah," he said.

The two girls turned around.

There in the doorway was Larry. He had four guards with him. All of them had guns. Big guns.

"Okay, boys," growled Larry through his grain sack. "Let 'er rip."

GETAWAY

A guard pointed a gun at them and fired. The shot ricocheted off Jasper's helmet. The girls had dropped to the floor.

The mule, hearing the shot, panicked. Suddenly it was galloping toward the guards.

The guards said things like "Whoa!" and "Ouch!"—unhelpful, brief, one-syllable things. They tumbled backward in a heap.

Jasper, Katie, and Lily ran over them, stepping over their limbs.

Larry was picking himself up off the floor. He screamed, "Guards!"

"Larry's grain sack!" panted Katie as they ran. "It's off partway!"

Jasper looked back. "He's—his teeth! What is that? By dumpkin, what is it?"

They kept running.

"They've seen my mouth!" yelled Larry. "Get them!"

The guards slowly stood.

The mule was stomping down the hallway. The kids were right behind it.

Larry and the guards ran after them.

The guards turned the corner and were confronted by an empty hallway with many doors.

Slowly the guards paced along the hallway, listening carefully at each door.

Larry fixed his grain sack.

"It will be hard to find those kids now," whispered one of the guards to another.

"Oh," said the other, "but you know what makes it really much easier? A supervisor standing there yelling 'Guards!' and 'Get them!' That's super. Thank goodness we have a guy like that on our side."

"What are you saying?" snapped Larry. "Are you saying something?"

"Nothing, boss," said one of the guards. "You just keep standing there, hollering 'Let 'er rip.' Fix your little grain sack. Maybe eat a snack bar. You're a great manager. That's why they pay you the big cashola."

"Miserable humans," muttered Larry. "I am so glad that my father married a . . ."

The guards all turned to look at him.

Larry folded his hands behind his back and rocked on his heels.

"Now that I've got your attention," he said, "carry on."

The guards kept creeping along the hallway, listening at all the doors.

"Boss," whispered one guard, "I can hear something in the conference room."

Larry nodded. "Break the door down. Like usual."

They kicked open the door and jumped in.

There was the mule, eating the strategic map of world domination.

And there were the kids, escaping through the opposite doorway.

The guards ran after them.

Oh, I don't know about you, but I really hate chase scenes. It's all just chase, chase, chase, up the staircase, down the staircase, *bang, bang, bang,* "Over this way," "No—that way," under the desk, over the chair, and you know that either they're going to get caught, or they're not. So why prolong the agony?

I'll just flat out tell you.

They made it to an old laundry chute.

"They're right behind us!" screamed Jasper. "Jump down the chute!"

"Jump?!?" said Katie. "Are you crazy?"

"Don't worry! My Titanium Bullet-Mobile is parked at the bottom. Five seconds from now, and we'll be blasting away, beyond the reach of Larry and his goons!"

They jumped. They screamed "Whooaaaa!" all the way down.

They landed in their seats—upside down but still, they landed.

"Good job, Jasper!" said Katie. "This is great! Let's get out of here!"

"No problems now, fellows!" said Jasper. He pulled off his helmet and pulled on his motoring goggles. "With the old Bullet-Mobile, we'll be off in a jiffy." He flicked a switch. "It's the first rocket-powered car! Rocket number one, engage! Rocket number two, engage!" He flicked another switch. The car started to move.

They were beside the old warehouse. They could see guards running out of the doors.

"Hurry!" pleaded Lily.

"Don't worry," said Jasper. "They'll never be able to follow us! Rocket number three, engage—and we're off!" The Bullet-Mobile rolled more quickly toward the street.

The roar of the engines was unbelievable. Like being inside a firework. Huge flames leaped out of the back of the car. Sparks splattered all over the stone walls and the pavement.

"Hold on to your hats, ladies!" cried Jasper Dash. "You're in for a wild ride! This futuristic buggy can attain speeds of up to thirty-five miles per hour!"

"Thirty-five?" said Katie.

"That's right," said Jasper proudly.

"Just thirty-five?"

"Yes indeed."

"Oh, great," groaned Katie, burying her head in the plush calfskin upholstery.

And behind them, guards poured out of the building.

GOONS ON WHEELS

Several of the guards had piled into a green Subaru station wagon and were swinging around corners after the Bullet-Mobile, firing their guns and changing rounds with their teeth.

Jasper expertly steered the rocket-powered car around fruit carts and pedestrians. Flames and smoke billowed out behind him. "We are gone in a flash!" He called backward into the wind, "Now—how do you like the tables turned, you gun-toting rapscallions?"

Katie said, "I wouldn't make fun of them too much until you reach the speed limit." She looked nervously backward. "You know, you can still go over twenty in a school zone."

"Katie, while your comments are well

meant, you should know that I would never put myself above the laws of the land and even *approach* the posted speed limit. I am a plucky yet principled youth, not a maniac daredevil."

"Jasper," called Lily. "Jasper?"

"Yes, Lily?"

"It might be better if we...uh...parked somewhere."

"Why, Lily?"

"Because the flames are kind of...visible. We got a big head start, but I think that they can see us because of the fire. Coming out of the back of the car."

"By jove!" said Jasper. "You may be right!"

He screeched around a corner. They were on a slope in a quiet neighborhood, on a tree-lined street.

Jasper turned off the engines and rolled down the hill. He pulled to the side of the road and kept rolling.

Lily, looking backward, saw the green Subaru station wagon fly past the end of the road.

Without the flames to alert them, the guards hadn't seen the car.

"Quick thinking," said Jasper.

"Now we can just sit and take a deep breath," said Katie. "Phew. That was a close one."

"I apologize for the slow speeds of my Titanium Bullet-Mobile," said Jasper. "I guess I haven't been keeping up with current trends. Also, I was forced to register it as an agricultural vehicle so I could drive it while I'm underage. As such, it is not allowed to go any faster than a tractor until I get a driver's license. Which will be some years from now." He sighed. "Dash it all!"

Katie stretched her arms. "Well, it wasn't a very successful mission. We didn't get the microfilms—I mean, the two-hundred-pound wax roll—with the secret stuff on it."

"No," said Jasper unhappily. "More's the pity."

"And they know we're spying on them now," said Katie.

"I feel as if this is somehow my fault," said Jasper even more unhappily.

"And if they figure out that it was Lily, then her dad will probably be in danger."

"Katie," said Jasper, "there are times when good friends enjoy a certain kind of silence."

"It's not a loss at all," said Lily quietly. "Now we know what we're up against."

"Goons with guns?" said Jasper. "That we knew before."

"No," said Lily. "We know much more than that. We saw part of Larry's face. Most of his mouth."

"It was really weird looking," said Katie.

"And I think that gives us a hint as to his whole ... you know, insane scheme," said Lily.

Her two friends turned to her.

"Okay," said Katie. "Now will you please explain?"

Lily tapped thoughtfully on the car door. "Let's go to dinner at the Aero-Bistro, and I'll tell you what I think."

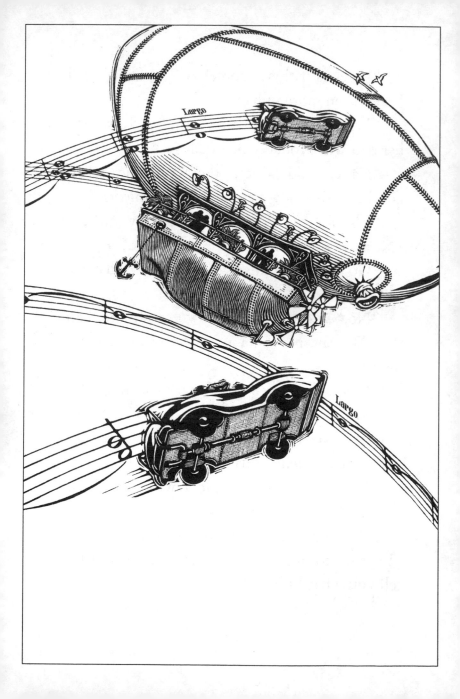

SOME OF THE THINGS
YOU CAN LEARN FROM
LARRY'S TEETH

That night the Aero-Bistro was floating in the middle of Jebb's Gorge, just outside of town. The trees on the cliffs were strung with lights. The dinner special was a hearty lobster-and-squash bisque. Music for the evening was supplied by members of a string quartet, who were playing energetic chords while sitting in the backseats of four speedsters that did daredevil jumps off the cliffs, flying past the Aero-Bistro. The music—one note per jump—was very solemn and slow, a little drowned out by the roar of the engines and the cries of the pit crews replacing tires.

"Well," said Katie, leaning back in her chair as a cello went by playing B-flat at a speed of about 170 miles per hour, "now maybe you'll tell us what that guy's weird mouth helped you figure out."

"To me it looked . . . It was like he didn't have teeth," said Jasper. "It was like thick white hairs instead of teeth."

"Up close," said Lily, "I'll bet they're wider than hairs. I'll bet they're made of the same thing as our fingernails."

"Hmm," said Jasper. "A whole mouth full of hangnails. No wonder he's so moody."

"No," said Lily. "It's not actually fingernails. It's called *baleen*."

"'Baleen,' huh?" said Katie.

Lily nodded.

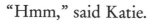

ba·leen [bay-leen] *n*   strips of hard fiber that occur in the mouths of certain whale species; used to strain out plankton, the microscopic organisms eaten by whales. Example: "It's so embarrassing going to the movies with my whale cousin and watching him try to eat popcorn through his *baleen*."

"Hmm," said Katie.

"And did you notice?" said Lily. "His skin was blue."

"So it was," mused Jasper. "As blue as the woad on a Celtic warrior's pinkie."

"Jasper," said Katie, "can you not use words like *woad* right now?"

Lily forged on. "One other thing about Larry. He pours brine over his head."

"So you're saying...," said Katie.

"I'm saying that Larry is a whale-human hybrid. He's a little of both. Remember when my dad said that he thought the company made stilts for whales? Well, he may not have been kidding. They may actually make stilts for whales..."

"So that the whales," said Jasper, catching on, "can invade the land!"

"Exactly!" said Lily.

"Dastardly!" cried Jasper.

"Whoaaaaaaaa!" exclaimed Katie.

They stared into space, uncertain of what to do with this terrifying news. The string quartet whizzed past, leaping between the limestone outcroppings.

"Why couldn't we have had one of *those* cars for our escape?" complained Katie.

"Why would we need a string quartet?" asked Jasper.

"I mean, those cars go over twenty miles per hour."

"But...they're not rocket powered," said Jasper, hurt.

"Jasper," said Katie, putting her hand on his wavy, heroic blond hair, "it's so sweet how you risk our lives for gadgets."

"I have a few things I want to ask my dad," said Lily, tapping her index finger on her teeth.

They all nodded solemnly. They looked out over the gorge and the trees strung with Chinese lanterns.

There is nothing better than friends working together against incredible odds. It is a great feeling. Some friends of mine and I, for example, once had to stop this jerk we knew from middle school who was trying to carve his face next to the presidents' on Mount Rushmore. He was the richest kid in school, and he had won a bunch of Italian stonemasons in a game of Go Fish. He and the stonemasons were headed down to Mount Rushmore in a bus.

You guessed it—he had won the bus in a karaoke competition with his mom. He had won singing "You Trouble Me Bigly."

I won't go into the whole thing, because I'm just trying to make a point that when you work on a project together with friends, and you're rushing around with climbing gear and scissors, and your friend Dana is explaining how to go up mountainsides, and your friend Lick is showing everyone how to disable a helicopter, and you're doing your part by writing personalized haiku for each of them, you get this intense feeling of love for your friends, and you come to admire them even more than you did before.

You start to think, *I would really hate it if*

they were injured or destroyed in an invasion of whales on stilts.

This is what Lily, Jasper, and Katie were all thinking.

Funny that they should be thinking that, though. Because later that very night ...

BRINE AND DINE

While the three kids met at the Aero-Bistro, Larry, hidden away in his secret laboratory, was lowering himself into a salt bath. He pulled off his mask, muttering, "And I would have gotten away with it, too, if it hadn't been for those meddling kids and their mule."

He leaned back in the bath. His skin was thick, slippery, and blue. His mouth was in a big scowl, and in the water his baleen glistened. He spoke to two of his head guards, who stood nearby. "We must find those children before they spread word of my plan. The one girl looked familiar—the one with the hair in her eyes and the handlebar mustache—but I can't quite place the face. It was quite an unmemorable face.

61

Somehow the mustache throws me off. But that other girl—I know I've seen her face somewhere ..."

He absently plucked at his baleen as if playing the harp.

"So they saw my face. My face!" He slapped the water angrily with his blue hands. Then, more quietly, he muttered, "My mother was a razorback whale. My father was a very lonely sailor. They were married in Barbados and lived a happy life together until ... But I won't talk about that. Then they bred me ... Me! ... A monster! Laughed at by all! Even by my cousin, my jerky cousin who now writes for the dictionary! The dictionary, do you hear? *I am a monster! Yes indeed!* But a monster who shall one day soon rule the earth!"

His voice echoed in the chamber.

The two guards stood against a wall.

Finally one of them said, "Do you, uh, want us to say anything? Or just listen?"

"Just listen. That will be fine." Larry stroked

his chin. "Aha! Yes! Eureka! That's it. I have got it. I know exactly who that meddlesome girl is. Her name is Katie something...Katie...Yes. I've seen her posters up...here and there..."

"You mean the one in your office, boss?"

"Yeah, okay? Yeah, the one in my office. It is my business, Rod, if I want to join the Horror Hollow Fan Club. Isn't it? Tell me, Rod. Tell me right now. Isn't that my business? So I like to read and improve my mind. So I like novels full of suspense and action. So I joined the Horror Hollow Fan Club. Okay?"

"Fine with me, boss."

"And that girl, that's where she's from— Horror Hollow. Her name is Katie Mulligan. See? Where would we be if I hadn't joined the fan club?" He clapped once. "Now here's what I want you to do. Look in the phone book for some Mulligans who live over in Horror Hollow. Send one of our operatives to her house. One of our *special* operatives."

"Yes, boss."

"I think you know what I mean by empha-sizing *special.*"

"Yes, boss."

"Big, you know...with the..." Larry winked and made a sound like something gigan-tic on stilts wreaking destruction on a suburban cul-de-sac.

"Yes, boss. You mean..." The guard stuck his fingers in his mouth and made the sound of something towering on stilts smiting an address in Horror Hollow, and dark smoke rising up to the unforgiving sky.

"That's it. See that she never tells a soul what she has seen here."

"Yes, boss."

"Now. Go!"

The guard turned and left.

Larry sat in his salt bath, thinking. "Very soon," he said, "*very* soon the years of planning will pay off. The world will be amazed at my power. Not much longer! Ha! Great! To think that soon I'll be..." He sank down and disappeared beneath the surface of the water.

Bubbles drifted up because he was still talking, still describing his fiendish schemes, though no one could hear or make out his words.

NIGHT. A BAY WITHOUT PEOPLE.

Picture a deserted cove. A dirt road runs right down into the bay. During the day people put their boats in here. It's a public launch. They zip around Smogascoggin Bay, waving to one another. Their skin looks shiny, and they drink pop.

But at night there's no one here. Picture that—people not being here. I know that's hard, because the minute I say "People," you start to picture them. You see all their striped bathing suits and their sunglasses, and they're waving at you. Well, you have to get rid of them. Remove them. Just leave a blank space where they were standing or sitting. The motorboat you're picturing fades away, the burr of its engine softly drifting off over the waves until it's gone. The water stills. The tide is slowly going out.

The smell of cocoa butter is replaced by the stench of night weeds.

The cooler full of brightly colored colas grows transparent....In its place the cans of cola are left, crushed and empty, on the beach in the blue of the night.

There are no bare feet anymore. Just footprints in the mud. No bathing suits. Nothing but the tide whispering in the salt marsh grasses.

The trees hang over the dirt road, swaying in the wind.

Far out at sea, a foghorn sounds.

It is not a foggy night, but the lighthouse keeper promised her grandson he could pull the horn once if he was good at dinner.

Everything is motionless, except the gentle shorthand of the lapping wavelets.

Then suddenly the water boils. Startled seagulls flap out of the marsh, squawking. Something is rising through the depths.

You know what it is.

Inch by inch it rises out of the sea. It has barnacles over its eyebrows. It is a great dark lumbering shape. It moves clumsily toward shore. It heaves itself up, towering. And it takes its first steps onto the land, exposed, for the first time, to the glare of moonlight.

An old fisherman is asleep against a stump. He spent the evening chasing saltwater eels. He hears a tremendous *crunch*—and awakens to see something he can't even describe striding over his beached dinghy, leaving it in ruins. He starts running. He vows never to drink diet cola again.

He runs, puffing, along the shore, away from the monster.

The monster stomps up the path, toward civilization.

Toward Horror Hollow. And Katie Mulligan.

HE LOVES HIS MOTHER

But wait.

Larry's story is a sad one. I cannot really go on to the terrifying scene that is about to occur—the breathtaking confrontation—until I stop to shed a tear for the little boy that Larry used to be.

Come over to his desk. Not his desk at work but his desk at home, crammed full of his bills, a few photos of friends who betrayed him, his checkbook, receipts, order forms, and sheets of address labels he got for free from Easter Seals, which are now all stuck to themselves because of the water on his hands.

Go to that desk and slide out the bottom

drawer. There you will find a piece of paper folded up into thirds.

Unfold it.

It is empty except for one sentence—written in the middle of the blank page in a childish hand in blue crayon. A sentence full of the sadness of a child. It reads:

MY MOTHER IS A FISH.

At some point, the word *fish* was crossed out in pen; and over it was written, in a slightly older hand,

large aquatic mammal.

It is the correction that really breaks the heart.

You should always know your enemy.

Ray Like a Bat Out of Heck

"How was your day at work, Dad?" Lily asked, almost cowering at what the answer might be. She had just gotten home from the Aero-Bistro.

"Oh, pretty good. Pee-ritty good," said her dad, yawning. He kept cutting chives. He was making dinner.

"Anything interesting happen?"

"No. Nope. Well, some evil photocopier repairmen invaded and tried to steal the company mule, but other than that, nope."

They could faintly hear Lily's mom downstairs, singing along to pop songs while working out on the Thigh-er-sizer. She was singing a teen ballad out of breath. " 'Bad, stupid love! I try to rise above!/Bad, stupid you! It's time that we're through!'" She sang it very cheerfully, not paying much attention to the words.

"Honey," said Lily's father, "could you turn on a noisy appliance of some kind?" He flicked on the coffee grinder himself. "There. That's better."

Lily got out plates for the dinner table and opened the silverware drawer. She asked, "Dad, have you ever seen Larry's face?"

"No. Not his face, *per se.* Not *seen,* I mean, *seen* like with the eyes. He's a funny kind of guy, Larry."

"If I asked you, would you say that it's possible or impossible that…um…Larry is a half-human, half-whale mutant who eats plankton through his baleen-filled mouth?"

Her dad thought about it for a few moments. He turned up the burner on the stove and threw chives into a frying pan. Finally he said, "Possible, I guess. That would explain the weird sighting a few months ago."

Lily's eyes popped wide open. "What 'weird sighting'?"

"One sec. Let me turn off the coffee grinder." He shut it off. Immediately the kitchen was filled with a creepy, decaffeinated silence. Lily's father narrowed his eyes and told his tale.

"Well, a few months back, my coworker Ray was working late at night. He had a report to finish, so he ordered Chinese takeout and stayed at the office. As you can imagine, that office is pretty spooky when no one else is around. It's just a big empty brick building then, filled with all kinds of empty rooms and corridors where someone could hide. I don't like to think about it.

"So Ray's sitting there, and he hears this dragging sound out in the hall. It sounds like someone dragging something. He thinks, *That's funny... What would someone be dragging at this hour? Usually everything that needs to be dragged gets dragged before five forty-five.* So he goes to the door and looks out.

"Nothing in the hallway. And now the footsteps and the dragging are farther away.

"So he starts creeping down the hallway.

"He comes to one of the laboratories. They're real spooky at night, because they're filled with things someone could hide behind. So someone could be in the same room as you, easy, without you even knowing. They could just be crouching there, watching you. So when he gets to the lab, Ray calls out, 'Hello?' There's no answer. He goes, 'Hello?' again.

"This time a door on the other side of the room slams.

"He runs over there and through the door. And there he sees this awful ... this awful half-human, half-whale *thing* dragging its tail behind it, crouched over, fighting for breath, wearing swimming trunks. And it's stumbling toward this salt bath that Larry had installed in the plant.

"Ray is absolutely terrified. He doesn't even know what to do, so he panics and asks it to turn out the lights when it's done, and then he turns and runs back to his office. He was so frightened, he only stayed there in his office another two hours, finishing the report and copying and collating it and putting the copies into matching folders before he left in sheer terror. He hightailed it out of there like a bat out of heck."

"That must have been Larry!" said Lily. "He must have stayed away too long from the salt water and was trying to get back to it to, you know, revive himself!"

"I don't know what you have against Larry. If he wants to be a half-human, half-whale mutant, I don't think that's anybody's business but his own."

"But, Dad! He wants to take over the world!"

"We've already discussed this, young lady."

"He's going to lead an invasion!"

"Honey. Honey slug. Listen. I've told you before. All our company makes is stilts for whales, and a few accessories that go with them. There is absolutely nothing strange about it. And you'll see. Three days from now is our product launch."

Lily felt her face go pale. "What does that mean?" she asked.

"Well, we're done with the product, the whale stilts, so in three days Larry is going to release the product. That's probably what he meant when he said, 'Take over the world.' He meant that we're going to dominate the whale-stilt world, the whole market for whale stilts. Starting in three days."

"Dad! That must be when he's going to un-leash his whole whale army! On all of us!"

"His 'whale army'? Now that sounds a little silly, Lily, doesn't it? Just because whales will be able to walk on stilts doesn't mean that they're going to be up in arms—if you'll, heh, pardon the expression."

"Dad!"

"Lily, that's a *whale* of a story! Get it?"

"I've got to go to Katie's house after dinner. She and I have to talk."

"Okay," said Lily's father. "Just make sure you finish your homework."

Homework! thought Lily. How could she concentrate on homework when in three days an army of tall bloodthirsty land-borne whales could be stalking the countryside, looking for revenge?

Practically speaking, that would probably mean Lily's math test would be canceled, anyway.

A Quiet Night In

Meanwhile, over in Horror Hollow, Katie's mom peeked in her room and said, "Your dad and I are going out for the evening. Will you be okay?"

"I don't know," said Katie. "I guess so."

"What's wrong, honey?"

Katie shrugged. "I think I'm just jumpy."

Her mother nodded sympathetically. "I know. Because of that whole thing last week with the liver-eating scarecrow."

"Yeah, and the psychokiller. And the singing bats. And the serpents. And the Civil War soldiers. And my evil double from the other dimension."

Her mom came in and tousled her hair. "It all kind of wears you down after a while, doesn't it, honey?" she said. "But your dad and I have dinner plans with the Wilsons. We have a lot to talk over with them. They're on a committee to repair the sewage drains after the mind-worms."

"You couldn't eat here?"

"No, I'm afraid that we already made reservations. But I made you some Rice Krispies Treats, and there's garlic on the door, and you have your crucifix and ankh, right?"

"Yeah," sighed Katie.

"Alrighty," said her mother. She kissed Katie on the forehead. "Be good. Remember: in bed by ten, with the lights out and the room completely dark except for a ghostly sliver of moon creeping across the floor toward your bed."

After her parents left, Katie worked for a while on her homework. She had the math test coming up, and it felt good to go over some of the problems she hadn't got before. This time she felt like she really understood them.

So often when disaster is about to strike, we don't suspect a thing.

When Katie was done with her homework, she went down to watch a little TV. She sat in the living room on the sofa. She was watching some stupid sitcom. Whenever there were commercials, she'd flip to something else. Finally she gave up on watching the sitcom completely and just left the TV on the Spanish channel. When the commercials came on, she dug between the sofa cushions to see what change she could find.

She wasn't sure what first worried her about the windows.

She looked up. The windows were completely dark. There was no sign of motion.

She got up and walked over to a window. She touched her fingers to the glass. She peered through.

Nothing.

There were windows all around the living

room. She looked through all of them. She couldn't see anything but the front and side yards.

She felt a prickling at the back of her neck. Slowly she turned.

Nothing.

But in the next room, in the dining room—there were windows there, too. If someone was standing outside, in the bushes, in the dark, Katie would be visible. Very visible. Well lit. Inside. She would be seen through the window, down the hall, and through the open doorway, standing stock-still, looking out blindly into the darkness.

There could be someone there.

Katie walked carefully into the dining room. Nothing to fear but windows.

They were black with the suburban night of Horror Hollow.

She rested her knuckles against the glass and looked through. There were the bushes, where she had pictured someone standing. There was no one standing there. In the neighbors' yard, there was a turtle sandbox.

The eyes were behind her.

She swiveled. Something flickered past the living room windows.

She started lowering the shades in the dining room. She would shut all the shades in the house. At least that way, no one would be able to see her. She could fight them more effectively if they didn't know where to find her.

She looked up. There was motion in the room with her—

No—only a mirror. It was just her own reflection in the mirror over the sideboard. Katie backed toward the wall. Her back was pressed against it.

She heard a ratcheting.

The front door.

She realized, *It might not be locked.*

She galloped across the room and saw the knob slowly turning. Breathing in gasps, she grabbed the lock and twisted it. She pulled the chains across.

Now there was no sound from the outside. Nothing. Whoever it was, was biding his or her time. Waiting for Katie to open the door and look to see who was there.

Someone or something was trying to get in. Seriously trying to get in. Other doors. She thought about other doors.

Katie ran into the living room. Yanked the drapes shut. The kitchen door. Was it locked?

She headed back.

No, no—she knew it was locked. She had locked it earlier, when she took out the garbage. Time to call the police. She started up the stairs toward the phone.

As she reached the top of the stairs and was about to turn the corner to go to her room to phone, she realized that there was a huge window at the end of the upstairs hallway. Someone in the backyard would be able to see

her, frightened, running for the phone. Someone would know just where she was.

Nothing else for it. She had to get to the
phone.

She peeked around the corner.

There was the window. Nothing. Just a dark,
midnight blue.

Then the blue moved.

And revealed a red glaring floating eye.

If you're enjoying this thrilling Katie Mulligan story, you'll want to rush out and stuff your arms, pockets, and mouth with more . . .

Horror Hollow™ Books

"Just a little bit kooky— but incredibly spooky!"

__ Horror Hollow #230   **Hear No Evil**
__ Horror Hollow #231   **Earwigs!!!**
__ Horror Hollow #232   **May the Best Brain Win**
__ Horror Hollow #233   **Mob-zilla—An Offer You Can't Refuse**
__ Horror Hollow #234   **Green Eggs and Human**
__ Horror Hollow #235   **Detention—Forever!!!!**
__ Horror Hollow #236   **The Skull Beneath the Skin**
__ Horror Hollow #237   **Yours for the Axing**
__ Horror Hollow #238   **Earwigs 2!!!**
__ Horror Hollow #239   **There's Something Nasty in the Locker Room**
__ Horror Hollow #240   **Tic-Tac-Die**

While you're at it, join Katie's fan club and get lots of cool Horror Hollow™ stuff—like a Horror Hollow ghost hunter's badge and a poster of Katie being eaten by trees!

Buy all 240 Horror Hollow™ volumes and get a free membership!

Horror Hollow™—your vacation to terror!

Available at a fine bookstore near you![*]

---

[*]Except in the contiguous United States, Hawaii, Alaska, Bermuda, Canada, the United Kingdom, and where void and prohibited by injunctions against the advertising and sale of imaginary merchandise.

An Eye for an Eye

The eye was looking for her, looking at her, a huge eye, a single eye.

Katie screamed and leaped backward and flattened herself against the wall of the stairwell.

A second later the window exploded. A blast of red light filled the hallway. She heard her sister's graduation photograph blow up as well as the pictures of Uncle Luke getting Kool-Aid dumped on his head by that nurse.

A whale. It was a whale, a walking whale on stilts, with deadly laser-beam eyes. Her grandpa had always said this time would come.

What to do? She started running down the stairs—but then thought again and scrambled back up.

She peeked around the corner.

There was the eye—*VLAM!*—blasting away at her again. Chunks of plaster and wood flew through the air. She stumbled backward and slid down several steps. She crouched there. She didn't know which way to go.

Suddenly she heard an ominous crunching.

The shrubs. The whale was pacing along on its stilts through the shrubs, trying to find a different window to shoot through.

He was heading for the back. Katie darted down the stairs and headed for the front door. It was time to make a break.

She reached the bottom of the steps and heard the whale thrashing around in the backyard. She was almost to the door—

—when someone started pounding on it.

Someone was trying to get in.

THE SWEET SOUND OF
LASER FIRE

"Katie!" Lily yelled. "Katie! Open up! There's a giant whale on stilts outside your house!"

"Oh, thanks," said Katie with some sarcasm, unlocking the door and opening it. "I thought it was just squirrels going after the hummingbird feeder."

Lily rushed in. "I called the police from your neighbor's house."

"They're on their way?"

Lily looked troubled. "They didn't seem too...uh...when I said..."

"They didn't believe you, did they?"

"Well—"

Suddenly there was a loud laserlike noise*

---

*You know what I mean. I'm talking about *vooooeeeeep—KPCHKWOW!!!*

88

from upstairs, and plaster shot down the stairway.

"He's getting in!" shouted Katie.

"I have a plan!" Lily shouted back.

"Okay! Whatever you say!" shouted Katie.

Lily ran into the dining room and threw open the drapes. She opened the window and shouted, "Over here! Over here!"

"What are you doing?" Katie exclaimed. "Don't open the drapes!"

"Help me with that!" said Lily, running to the other side of the dining room.

"What? My mom's collectible *Streetcar Named Desire* plates?"

There was a stomping noise from outside. Bushes crushed beneath huge iron cuffs. The whale was getting closer.

"No! The mirror!"

They ran to the mirror above the side table and lifted it down. Katie was starting to catch on. She and Lily knelt behind the mirror, facing the windows, and yelled through the open window, "Here! Over here, you stupid whale!"

Suddenly the whale's huge face dipped down into view: his red glowing eyes, his blue-gray hide, his big snarling baleen mouth. On his head was a kind of metal cap with an antenna.

The red eyes started to sparkle.

"He's going to shoot!" said Katie.

The girls ducked.

The whale fired his laser-beam eyes. ~~The girls felt the jolt as the laser beam bounced off the mirror.~~

Of course the girls didn't feel the jolt as the laser bounced off the mirror, because lasers are

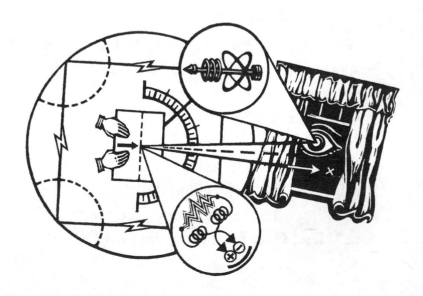

just light. This story is highly scientific, and I would never mislead you. I want to depict whale eye-laser technology as accurately as possible.

Instantaneously the laser doubled back on itself, a continuous stream of light—using all the standard oculo-incendiary prohulsifiers and megegolisms that you'd expect—and it flashed through the air, *searing the whale itself*!

The girls heard him screech in pain, in that way whales do. He had been badly burned.

He fired again. Once again the girls didn't feel the impact of the lasers on the mirror. Once again the laser beams ricocheted—one hit the whale full in the snout, and the other one flew off and smashed a wall-mounted soup tureen depicting Marlon Brando as Stanley.

The whale bellowed in pain and anger.

Lily and Katie dared now to look over the top of the mirror.

The whale was staggering. They could see his tall metal stilts, big hydraulic things, stumbling around the lawn.

"We got him!" shouted Katie.

The whale was headed back down the driveway. He was in retreat.

The girls ran to the front door. They opened it. The whale was jogging down the road away from the house, lightly on fire. Cars swerved to avoid his huge sticklike electrical legs. A driver rolled down a window and screamed, "Stupid whale! Whadaya think this is, the Bering Strait?"

The girls breathed a sigh of relief.

For the moment they were safe.

It is a general rule that things on stilts never strike the same place twice. Except some clowns, when you don't pay them back for some stupid old Dutch paintings they bought you.

But that's another story.

KATIE MULLIGAN AND THE CURSE OF THE JAGUAR

It wasn't long before the authorities arrived. Even though the police didn't believe in things like giant walking laser whales, the Horror Hollow Neighborhood Association was very used to vampires, madmen, flying saucers, and Bigfeet—so a walking whale really wasn't much of a stretch. Some of the people from the Neighborhood Association came over, with blankets and hot cocoa, to see if Katie was all right and to help clean up some of the mess. The house was scorched and many of the windows had shattered. A wall upstairs lay strewn across the bedroom.

Katie and Lily sat in their blankets in the jumbled living room, talking.

Lily said, "I came over to tell you that in three days, Larry is going to release his whale army."

"Oh no . . . ," said Katie. "What'll we do?"

Lily thought hard. "We're going to have to figure out some weakness of the whales."

"What about using more mirrors?"

"We'd have to cover everything with mirrors to be safe. There must be some other way." Lily frowned, thinking hard.

Several men came in. They were thin and nervous.

"Oh no," said Katie. "It's the writers from Harcourt. They're here to find out what happened so they can write the next Horror Hollow book."

"Miss Mulligan?" one said. "We'd like to find out a few details to use in the upcoming book."

"Hi," Katie said. "We're kind of in the middle of a conversation right now."

"We'd like to get started writing," said the writer. "Could you just fill us in on a few details?"

"Miss Mulligan, how did you fight off the whale?"

"Miss Mulligan, why are whales out to get you?"

"Miss Mulligan, when you crept up the stairs, was it *timidly* or *intrepidly*?"

The writers waited. One had his laptop computer open and turned on. His fingers quivered over the keys.

"It wasn't me who figured out how to chase off the whale," said Katie. "It was my friend Lily."

The writers looked from one girl to the other.

"Okay," said one. "That's fine. But a little bit confusing for the reader, because you're the hero. So for the purposes of the series, we'd like to make it be you. And Lily helped. But was carried away by the whales to their secret underwater hideout."

"In the ruins of the *Titanic*," said another writer. "Where there's a room full of gold bricks."

"Stolen from the Duchesse de Désastre," said the first writer.

"And the whales are in cahoots with the killer bees coming up from Mexico," said the third writer. "Because of the Aztec curse."

"The Curse of the Jaguar," explained the first writer triumphantly.

"But this whole thing started with Lily!" said Katie. "Tell them, Lily!"

But Lily just looked uneasy and shy.

"Go on!" said Katie. "Tell them about going to work with your dad!"

"It's fine," said Lily.

"Great," said one man.

"Super," said another.

"Exactly," said the third.

And the one with the laptop started typing quickly.

One of the writers explained to Katie, "Your friend Lily doesn't have the pizzazz you do. The presence." (Lily turned her face away from them. She suddenly didn't want to be in the room.) The man continued, "She doesn't have that special *oomph*. She doesn't have that glossy girl-glamour that's important for our readers. For example, when a writer, a good writer, wants to write a description of his main character, he wants to be able to say something like, 'She looked in the mirror at her pretty brunette hair and her thin five-foot-one-inch frame.' *Not* 'She looked in the mirror at her squat five-foot-one-inch frame and her flat brown hair that completely covered her eyes, except when she blew on it diagonally.'"

"Tell you what," said one of the writers. "We could maybe work in your friend Lily if she could be a comic sidekick. You can have a squat, flat-haired comic sidekick." He asked Lily, "Can you tell jokes?"

(Lily wanted there to be a hidden place under the rug where she could lie without moving and just listen, unseen by anyone—ever.)

"That's insulting," said the third writer angrily. "I can't believe he even said that. I apologize. Here's a better idea: How about we have Lily have some kind of makeover partway through the book. Like, after everyone thinks that she's just quiet and her hair is always over her eyes, somehow her hair gets pulled back—and suddenly she's really sexy, and everyone's like, 'Whoa, Lily! When you completely change your look, you're beautiful!'"

"Gotcha!" exclaimed one of the writers.

"There's the ticket!" cried another.

Katie stood up and pointed at the door. "Get out!" she yelled. "We have just been attacked by a whale with laser-beam eyes, and I do not need you saying stupid things about my friend who just saved my life!"

"Touchy, touchy," said one of the writers.

"Werewolves getting to you?" said another.

"Someone's tangled with one too many mind-sloths," said the third, closing up his laptop.

"We'll be in touch," they said, and left.

Lily was sitting on the coffee table, shuffling her tennis shoes in the pile of the rug.

"Don't let them bother you," said Katie.

"I'm not bothered," Lily said. She turned her face away.

"Yes, you are."

"I'm okay."

"You're crying." Katie reached over and tugged gently on Lily's hair. "Hey."

Lily turned back around. She shrugged without words.

OPERATION AMBERGRIS
OR
CALL ME FISHTAIL

"Thar she blows . . . up everything that stands in the path to world domination!"

It looks like it will be a quiet night in for Katie Mulligan—but it's never just a quiet night in for Katie Mulligan! Especially not when her neighborhood, peaceful Horror Hollow, is being ransacked by a pod of laser-eyed whales! Now Katie must battle the evil whales absolutely alone, without the help of any friends at all, and come up with ingenious ways to defeat them—by herself!—if she's going to get back the gold contained in the sunken ship stolen from the infamous Duchesse de Désastre and stop the killer bees before they call down the feared . . .

Curse of the Jaguar!

"They don't know what they're talking about," said Katie. She put her arm around Lily. "You're the hero. You're the one who figured out this whole plot against the world by Larry. You're the one who figured out that Larry was a half-whale, half-human whatsit."

"Hybrid."

"Yeah. You're the one who figured out what his teeth really mean. And you're the one who just saved my life by figuring out what to do with the mirror."

Lily looked in the mirror at her squat five-foot-one-inch frame and her flat brown hair that completely covered her eyes, except when she blew on it diagonally.

"That's okay," she said. "It's your story."

"*No*—" said Katie. "It's *your* story. You have to realize that it really is. It's only when people realize that the story can be about them that they can start to change things."

Lily said glumly, "We have a lot to change. By three days from now."

"Exactly," said Katie. "And if you keep believing that this is Jasper's story or my story, you won't be ready to give everything to the story and save us all from the stilt-walking laser-beam whales."

Lily nodded. "What are we going to do?" she asked.

Katie flicked her hard on the arm. "It's *your* story. You decide."

"Well," said Lily. "We should learn about the weaknesses of whales."

"Yeah," said Katie. "We can go to the library."

"Or to an oceanographical institute."

"A what?"

"A place that studies the sea."

"Yeah!" said Katie.

"And we should ask my dad for more details about the stilts and the accessories. He might have heard other things that we can use against the whale army."

"Good idea!" said Katie.

"And we should figure out where they're going to come onto land first. If we can pinpoint that," said Lily, getting excited, "we could be there waiting for them . . ."

"Now you're planning!" said Katie. "See? This is great!"

Lily smiled shyly. "So you'll share the story?" she said. "Not that I need my own story."

"Everyone needs their own story," said Katie. "This one is yours."

Lily nodded awkwardly. "I'm glad I have someone to share it with," she said.

"Thanks," said Katie, grinning and resting her head against Lily's. "I'll remember that when we're both being fried by a humpback whale with ray-gun eyes."

THOUGHT CONTROL

The next day, when Lily's father was driving her to a dentist's appointment, she asked him, "Do you remember when I talked to you about the stilts for whales? How you told me that there were other accessories that went with them?"

"Lily," said her father, "this isn't about this whale 'invasion' again, is it?"

Lily didn't answer.

Her father sighed. He took his hand off the gearshift and patted her on the neck. "I realize that it must be hard being friends with Jasper and Katie, because they're so famous for their adventures. But that's no reason to make things up. That's no reason to start seeing conspiracies in everything. Okay, honey toad?"

"Just . . . what are the other accessories?"

"Nothing big, honey. Nothing worth talking about. Just laser implants in their eyes and a spray bottle that keeps them wet. That's all. And a kind of metal hat with an antenna that controls their thoughts from a remote location."

"What remote location?" asked Lily quickly.

"I don't know, Lil. Probably the laboratory. It's all perfectly straightforward."

"Have you heard anything about where whales are getting these things, uh, put on them?"

"I think over near the factory, out somewhere in Smogascoggin Bay. That's where they hitched up the prototypes. You know who you should ask about this? My pal Ray, who works with me. He could tell you all about this." Lily's dad nodded. "Except he was taken out of the office a few days ago with his hands tied behind his back and a bandanna tied as a gag on his mouth." Her father thought for a second. "Huh. He hasn't been in to work since. I wonder if he has the flu."

Lily felt like her hands were freezing to the seat. "Dad," she said, "could you not go to work today?"

"This is ridiculous, Lily. I'm not in any danger. We're going to have our launch in two days."

"It's not a launch; it's a whale invasion."

"Not another word!" said her father. "I'm sick of this! Okay, Lily? *Enough is enough!*"

Lily didn't know what to feel—terrified or angry. Being yelled at always made her shrink up inside. She sat there playing with the lock on the car door, frowning, trying not to cry.

But there was one thing she'd gotten out of the conversation, she realized. She had to tell Katie and Jasper about what she had found out. This new piece of news—that the whales were remote controlled—might be the key to defeating them. If only they could break that remote control's power over the whales' thoughts and actions . . .

When Lily got to the dentist's, she immediately asked where there was a pay phone. She ran to the corner and dialed Jasper's number.

Jasper picked up the phone in his laboratory. He was trying out some new springed shoes.

"Jasper?" said Lily. "The whales have metal hats put on them to control their minds, and lasers for eyes. I think that these things are being put on them someplace out in Smogascoggin Bay."

Jasper said,

    "Lily, it's   hard to

              kind of   pay attention

with these   on. One   second.

          spring shoes   durned

"Ah, that's better. Now, as you were saying."

Lily told him what she'd discovered.

They talked over their plan of action. They decided that Katie and Lily would go over to the Smogascoggin Oceanographical Institute and see what they could find out about whales. Jasper said that he would go out in his Marvelous Subaquatic Zephyr to see if he could spot any whales gearing up for battle on the ocean floor of the bay. While Lily talked on the phone, she watched people making appointments with the dentist's receptionist.

Suddenly it hit her: If she and her friends didn't do something, the appointments would never happen. Things scheduled for Tuesday would never come to pass. But people all around her were going on like normal, not knowing that everything was about to change.

Lily pictured the dentist's office and all the buildings around it as just a pile of gray bricks, scattered with drills and dentures, as if the rubble was hungry and openmouthed and would snap up passing flies.

Lily was such a nice person, it didn't even occur to her that a vision of the dentist's office destroyed should have actually cheered her up.

SONGS WITHOUT VOCAL CORDS

Later that day Lily and Katie went over to the oceanographical institute. They learned a lot about whales. They learned that whales survive underwater through various means, such as a surplus of oxygen-storing myoglobin in the whale's muscle tissue. They learned that whales make noises but have no vocal cords. They learned that the blue whale—the largest animal ever to exist—can weigh up to two hundred tons. The heart of one giant blue whale weighed about fifteen hundred pounds. They learned that most baleen whales eat euphausiids, copepods, and amphipods. They learned that the song of the humpback whale can last up to thirty-five minutes.

But they didn't learn anything specifically about combating walking whales with laser-beam eyes.

So let's leave them behind.

Meanwhile, far below the waters of the bay, a fake boulder slid aside and Jasper's Marvelous Subaquatic Zephyr slid out into the murky, polluted tides. His lights trawled the depths.

He headed cautiously toward the docks near the Abandoned Warehouse. He passed the piers, waving with green algae and speckled white with barnacles. He shone his lights over the bottoms of sailboats and motorboats, where they rocked on the waves above him. He passed two deep-sea divers giving each other a high five. They had just found a roll of quarters that had dropped off a harbor cruise.

Near the Abandoned Warehouse, the piers were broken and jagged. There were the remains of docks on the bottom, puffy with green slimy growth. Blind fish swam through fields of rusted cars and cans.

Jasper reached a brick wall—the back wall of

the Abandoned Warehouse. He knew that's what it was because it was painted on the bricks, in big letters: ABANDONED WAREHOUSE. Don't hit your head, if you're swimming! Turn aside!

There, right below the wall, was a secret berth—a big platform made of metal, with all kinds of industrial tools in brackets. The berth was shaped like this:

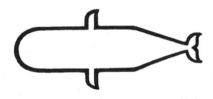

Jasper narrowed his eyes and scanned the sub's lights over the berth. There was no mistaking it—this was no flounder factory. This was definitely where the whales had been equipped with all of their "accessories," like the lasers and the mind-control helmets.

Now, he thought, *the trick is to find the whales themselves.*

He headed back out into the bay. For hours

he drifted back and forth, marking his path on a chart. He saw great boulders and old decaying trees. He puttered by manta rays. No whales, though.

At dinnertime he surfaced briefly to eat a sandwich. He opened his hatch and sat above water, munching on ham and cheese, sipping a wonderful tall glass of chocolate Gargletine Brand Patented Breakfast Drink, which left him feeling healthy, heroic, and refreshed. Why, every household should have a canister of Gargletine—fortified with seventeen essential nutrients found in no other foodstuff! Give it a try, moms of America, and you'll see why it's called "Pluck in a Bucket."

As he was sitting there, enjoying the great, sweet, laminated taste of Gargletine, he noticed something on the horizon.

Smoke.

No, not smoke. It was a kind of strange fog, rising from the water. It obscured the little pine-covered islands in the bay. It drifted up toward the moon.

No, not fog. It blew across his face. It was warm. He dropped his sandwich. "Steam," he said. "Steam! From the lasers! By george!"

Jasper scrambled below, clanged shut the hatch, and threw the Zephyr into Full Speed Ahead. It chugged swiftly through the darkened waters. Peering through his Aquatic Night Goggles, Jasper shut off the lights. His night goggles detected heat, instead of light. In total darkness his vessel shot past rocks and wrecks. He saw them through the goggles as dim purple shapes, lit by the bright green of living things— fish, clams, and sea anemones.

And finally, whales. Yes, he'd found the whales.

There were a huge number of them. Above, the surface of the water was roiling with the motion of them all, bubbling beneath the moon. They were circling around something he couldn't make out . . . Something purple with lots of swirls and curves . . . (He squinted.) . . . Something with many arms . . .

A squid—the natural enemy of the whale!

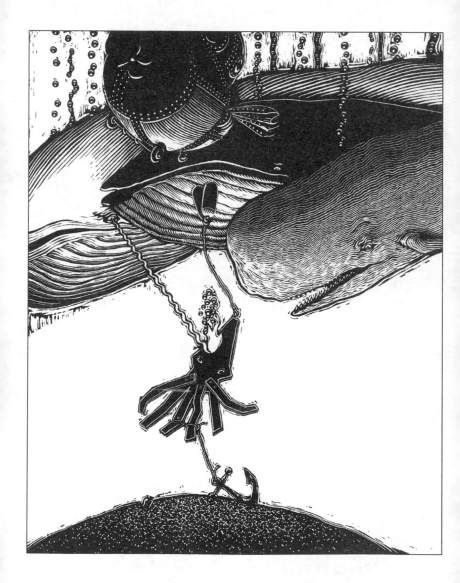

But there was something strange about the squid.... Living things showed bright green in Jasper's goggles. The squid was purple. Was it dead?

No, he realized. Not dead. It wasn't real. It was a target.

A bright light flashed. The whales were using a wooden stand-up squid for target practice. They were training themselves to use their eye lasers.

It was the heat from the lasers that had made the clouds of steam.

Jasper stayed well away from the whales. He didn't want to be detected. With so many of them, they would be able to crush his Zephyr like an aluminum can.

He had seen all he needed to. The whales were getting ready for war.

Quietly he backed his ship away from them. He headed toward shore.

WHALE CONTROL TO MAJOR TOM

On the way home from the oceanographical institute, Lily and Katie stopped at the police station.

I don't think I need to tell you how this conversation went.

Have you ever told the police that your house has been pillaged by whales? And then mentioned that tomorrow whales will invade the town?

In Lily and Katie's experience, the police responded by saying things like:

"What do you mean exactly by 'invasion'?"

"The whales," explained Katie, "are going to invade."

"Can I tell you a story, girls?" The police officer leaned back and rested his heels on his computer keyboard. He said patiently, "In the nineteen-sixties there was something called the British Invasion. But no British people really *invaded* us. It was called an *invasion,* but all that happened was a lot of British bands sold a lot of records in the United States."

"So you're saying," said Katie, "that really these whales are just going to release a lot of hit singles."

"Don't get fresh," said the police officer. "I'm saying that just because there was something called the British Invasion doesn't mean you should be afraid of British people. Except maybe the singer David Bowie, because he has those weird eyes. See what I mean? The British have never *invaded* America."

Lily mumbled, "What about during the War of 1812?"

"What about it?"

"They burned down Washington, D.C."

"Yeah." The policeman bit an apple. He chewed. "Do you girls ever do a sport?"

Let's end this painful interview and move on to something else.

Home Is in the Past

Lily couldn't sleep that night. She felt like little gyroscopes were spinning around in her wrists and ankles. She pulled back the covers and sat on the edge of her bed. Her room was dark. She could hear her father and mother talking quietly in the other room. No words, just muttering.

After a while Lily got up and padded down the stairs. She took the phone out of its cradle and went out on the porch. It was an early spring evening but not too cold. She sat on the wicker love seat and called her grandmother in Decentville.

"It's me," said Lily when her grandmother answered.

"Hello, beauty," said her grandmother. "It's eleven. That's when I watch my surfing videos."

"Grandma," said Lily, "there's something awful that's going to happen."

"What is it, darling?" said her grandma. "I'm going to go into the living room and sit down." Lily could hear a door slam on the other end of the phone. With a puff her grandmother plopped down on the sofa. "It's an invasion of some kind, isn't it?"

"Whales," said Lily.

"Oh, honey," said her grandmother. "At least the waiting is over."

Lily told her about what had happened so far. (If you're interested, you can go back to the beginning of the book and read all the way through to this point again.)

When Lily was done with her story, she said, "What am I going to do?"

"Why don't you fight them with your magic sword?"

"I don't have a magic sword."

"In the world of make-pretend, you can have anything you want, darling."

Lily felt tears gather in her throat. "Grandma, this isn't pretend."

Her grandmother didn't argue. "I wish games could go on forever," she said soothingly. "I remember, Lily…" She laughed.

Lily loved the sound of her grandmother's chuckle. She held the phone closer to her ear.

Her grandmother said, "The games we played when I was little lasted for days. We would be running around in the fields down by Tinker's Point like crazy people. We would hide in the grass. We always pretended we were food. Myrtle D. was ketchup. I was a side of bacon. We jumped off the rocks, being food, and I'm afraid we bumped up our knees sometimes."

Lily smiled.

"I remember the fireflies always being out," said her grandmother, "but probably that was only once or twice." Sadly, she added, "You know how, when you're remembering, you put beautiful things everywhere? You spread them out, and they fill the whole memory. Even if there weren't fireflies every night we played there, those were firefly times, Lily."

Lily just sat on the wicker and listened to her grandmother. She had curled up so that her knees were under her chin. Even just the sound of her grandmother's voice made her feel quiet and safe.

"Everyone wants to get back to the place they know best," said Lily's grandmother. "When you are old, though, sometimes that place is not just far away on the map but far away in time. How do you get to home, then, when home is in another era?"

Lily said, "I don't know, Grandma."

But something was clicking in Lily's brain. *Everyone wants to get back to the place they know best.*

"Grandma . . . ," she said. "Grandma, I think you might have given me an idea."

"That's sweet, darling," said her grandmother. "I was a little worried that you had fallen asleep or were calling from the john. Your cousin Sid does that, you know. He goes to the bathroom with the phone. I'm his granny; I can tell. Sometimes he grunts while he's talking."

"You've really helped me, Grandma."

"Can I say the other thing about Sid? He can't figure out how my front door works. Whenever he visits he goes around to the side, so he won't have to admit it."

They talked for a little while about Sid—talking like two girls about a boy—and Lily, curled in the wicker love seat, smiled for the first time in a while.

Finally she had a plan.

[   ]

The next day—the day before the whales invaded North America—Lily, Jasper, and Katie had a powwow over breakfast at the Aero-Bistro.

"It's deuced difficult to do anything," said Jasper, "when we can't convince any adults to help us."

Katie groaned, "No one will believe us."

Lily looked around carefully at the other diners and the android waiters. She whispered, "I think...Okay...I think I have a plan. Something we can try, anyway."

"Top-notch, Lily!" said Jasper. "But there's no need to whisper."

"Well—" started Lily.

"No need to whisper," declared Jasper, "because I just invented *these.*" He lifted up three metal masks with no eyeholes and what looked like bicycle horns coming out of where the mouth and ears would be. "They're Secret Planning masks. You slip them over your head," he said, demonstrating, "and then when you talk about a secret plan, only other wearers of a mask can hear."

Katie lifted one off the table and looked at it uncomfortably. "Wow, Jasper," she said. "These sure do have . . . a lot of rivets."

"Just a little something I cooked up," said Jasper proudly.

"Wouldn't it be easier for Lily just to keep her voice down?" Katie suggested.

"Come along! Give it a try!" said Jasper.

They all put on the masks. Their faces now were gray, with bicycle horns coming out of their mouths and ears.

"Hokay," said Katie. "Let's roll."

"Now, Lily, you just tell us the plan like you would normally," said Jasper. "We'll be able to hear perfectly, but no one else will be able to."

"I just ... talk?"

"Right-o."

"And the masks will just block out what we say when we're planning?"

"Check."

"Okay." Lily took a deep breath. "What I'm thinking is [

].”

"Hmm, yes," said Jasper. "Devilishly clever."

"[

                                          ]."
    "And you really think that's the best way to
get them to [   ]?" asked Katie.
    "[   ]," said Lily. "[

    ]." She used her hands to illustrate. "So
then when [

        ]."
    "And meanwhile," said Jasper, getting ex-
cited, "I could [

], and when they falter, I'll be there to [
                                          ]."

Katie asked, "Is anyone else finding that their breath is like pooling right under your chin? In this gross wet pool?"

"It's a fine plan, Lily," said Jasper.

"Does that mean we can take these off?" asked Katie.

Lily nodded her big clunky metal head.

"Good-o, then," said Jasper. "I'll order the Aero-Bistro androids to start [

]."

Lily said, "And I'll [

]."

"And Katie," said Jasper, "you can [

]."

Lily said, "But don't forget [   ]."

"Right-o," said Jasper. He lifted off his mask. The others lifted theirs off, too. Katie's face was all red and wet. She panted for air.

"Thank goodness," she said. "Planning makes it hard to breathe."

EXECUTION

If you want to guess their plan, you're welcome to.

Here's your clue: Later that afternoon Lily and Katie went to their favorite used-record store. It was a great used-record store, underground in the basement of a lounge-upholstery repair shop. There was fake tiger and leopard skin hanging from the walls, and all the pipes were painted red. The employees had hair that stuck out in different directions. Whenever Katie and Lily would go in to look for used CDs, someone would say, "Heya! It's the woosome twosome!"

Which didn't make any sense, but it's just nice to have people say something about you sometimes.

Katie and Lily looked through a big bin of vinyl records.

They chose a stack of them.

They went to the register. They paid.

They got $4.01 in change.

It was all part of the plan.

ATTACK

The next morning the sun rose around dawn. Nothing seemed unusual about the day: The dew was on the grass. People walked their dogs. The *Pelt Observer* featured stories about bake sales, weddings, and movies. Cereal boxes tipped toward bowls. Orange juice spilled on kitchen counters. Seagulls paced up and down the piles at the dump.

And yet, it was the day that whales invaded North America.

Jasper was talking to Lily on the phone before she left for school. Jasper called from his Marvelous Subaquatic Zephyr.

"I don't see hide nor hair of the whales down here. It will be a super ruckus, though, when we finally get to biff them."

"Did you go where you saw the squid target practice?"

"Yes indeedy. I'm there right now. Nothing left but the burned-up wooden squid. Rotten luck that you have to go to school. It would be ace if you and Katie could join me."

"I would stay home from school, but I'm in trouble with my dad. He found out I called the Coast Guard and the army and told them about Larry."

"I'll keep looking for our old pal Lares, and for his dastardly cetacean scoundrels. They must be on the move."

"I'll try to get out of social studies when they show up," said Lily. "So that we can get to ... you know ... carry out the plan."

There was a silence as they both thought about the trials of the coming day.

"I'm frightened," said Lily. "Really frightened."

"Tosh! Don't worry about a thing. Your plan is genius," said Jasper.

"I'm not so sure. If something doesn't work out—"

"What's wrong, Lily?"

"Everything could burn."

"We have faith in your plan."

_{"I know,"} said Lily in the smallest voice she had. _{"That's what's so frightening."}

"Lily," said Jasper, "we're going to do the best we can. Don't fear. Not everything will burn." There was silence on the line for a minute. Then he said, "For example, things that aren't flammable. Rocks, Lily."

Lily didn't say anything at her end of the phone. Jasper was altogether too sure of things.

"I've got to go," Jasper said. "I need to find these fellows before they emerge from the sea."

"All right," said Lily.

"Good-o, then. Over and out?"

"Be careful, Jasper."

"I will, Lily. You, too."

Lily hung up. She cleared the table of the breakfast dishes. Her father and mother were talking in the other room. Suddenly the phone rang. Lily picked it up and said hello.

"Oh, hey there, hey there," said a voice. "Is this little . . . Gefelty's little girl?"

"This is Lily," said Lily.

"Great. Great! This is your dad's boss, Larry. Is your dad there?"

"Sure," said Lily, fumbling with the phone. "Sure. Sure! I'll—I'll get him, then. While I go into the other room—how are you?"

"I'm good. Real good. How 'bout you?"

"And where are you? Are you at work?"

"Yeah, in a manner of speaking. Today's a big day for me. I have a lot of scrapple on my plate today. Hey—is your dad there?"

"I'm just—I'm getting him."

"That's great, 'cause I need to talk to him."

Lily had an idea—a way to find out where Larry was. "Can he call you back?" she said. "Are you at the warehouse?"

"Naw, naw. I'm not there right now. I'm in a yacht out in the harbor. Can I leave a message?

Where is he? Is he in the little boys' room? Because if so, could you just tell him to hurry up in there?"

"He's—I can give him a message."

"Tell him he doesn't need to come into work today. He and the rest of the team have done a great job, and they can take the day off. You know what I'd do, for instance? Maybe go horseback riding. Or skating, if he has access to an indoor rink."

"Okay. Thanks. Oh, incidentally, can you see the warehouse from there?"

"Uh, yeah. Why you ask? Is there something wrong with it?"

"No, no. I'm just—I'm just asking."

"Okay. Look, you take care of yourself. Have a good day in school or whatever. You know what I always found? In math the answer is usually seven. Alrighty. Keep in touch. Bye."

Larry hung up.

Lily ran into the living room. "Dad! Dad! Larry called and—"

Her mother and father were gaping at the TV. "Larry called?" her dad asked. "Thank goodness. That means he's safe."

"He said you don't have work today, and not to worry, and that your team did a good job."

"Of course we don't have work today," said her father, pointing at the TV screen. "The walls of the Abandoned Warehouse blew apart from the inside five minutes ago, revealing...I just can't believe this—there's a huge antenna and an army of walking whales!"

On the screen the whales were in formation, their eyes blazing, crunching through rubble.

Lily gasped. They were on the move.

The attack had begun.

SHELTER

If you have ever been present at a vicious attack by elevated sea animals, you'll know exactly what the people of Pelt felt like. I, for example, was unlucky enough to be working as a house-painter in Minneapolis that terrifying summer of the Manatee Offensive. That was awful. The sky was black with them.

Of course, the manatees weren't on stilts but wore small helipacks. The sound of those little helicopter blades chuddering in the summer air was overwhelming. It takes a lot to lift a mana-tee. You couldn't hear anything but the sound of them flying in their swarms while people honked their horns or ran for cover, weeping like babies.

I had a friend who had also lived through a

starfish attack, and during the manatee assault he pretty near fell apart. I had to keep shaking him. We were hiding in the frozen-food aisle of the Third Avenue Halt 'n' Buy. The manatees were buzzing around the parking lot just outside. My friend was getting hysterical. I finally slapped him. He blinked a few times and thanked me. He shook my hand. Then he stood and began, quite methodically, to jump up and down on boxes of Mrs. Paul's Fish Sticks.

Such are the peculiarities of the human psyche.

When Lily's father panicked, he really panicked. He was trying to coax her and her mother to go down to their "bomb shelter." The "bomb shelter" had been set up by a couple that had lived in the house in the 1960s.

"Come on!" said her dad. "We'll take the radio!" He stuffed his arms with magazines and cushions. "We can hear about what happens." He disappeared around the corner. "I'm going to grab some shirts!"

"Honey," said Lily's mother, "I'm not going down there."

"You'll be safe! You'll be safe down there! Come on!"

"All that's down there is the Ping-Pong table. How will the Ping-Pong table keep us safe?"

"We can play Ping-Pong until this whole thing blows over. And eat canned food."

"I'm not eating the canned food. The canned food expired during the cold war."

"Well, Lily, will you—"

Lily's dad skidded back into the room. Her dad and mom looked around.

"Lily?" they said. "Lily?"

But Lily was gone.

AIEEEEE!!!!

Lily was not in the living room because she had darted out the front door. She was already riding her bike down to Smogascoggin Bay. Everything was crazy down there. People flew past in their cars, usually 1950s cars, escaping. The whales had walked right through a vintage car rally. People fled past Lily. Many of the cars had fins, and were pink or green, and women in head scarves drove them, pointing backward and going, "AIEEEEE!"

Swaying above them all, outlined against the fresh morning sky, were the ominous shapes of the whales. They towered thirty feet high, their eyes glowing. They had spread their flukes.

They drooled from their wet baleen. They bared their teeth (those that had them).

Lily stopped on her bike and stood for a second at the crest of a hill. She stared with horror at the scene of destruction in the valley before her.

The huge mammals had stomped through the center of town. Behind them, down near the bay, was the business district of Pelt, the streets rucked like rugs with whale stilt prints. On the site of the Abandoned Warehouse was a giant pyramid-shaped antenna. Lily could just barely see the radio waves spreading out from it in circular ripples.

The whales did whatever the radio tower commanded. They stepped on used car dealerships and a putt-putt golf course.

The town was behind them; they were heading across the pasturelands of outermost Pelt. They burned down trees in a trice with their laser-beam eyes. They stalked in rows through the countryside.

The cows were panicked. People in farm-houses screamed from their windows. Families were in Ford trucks, banging past Lily on dirt roads. Dogs barked crazily.

Lily stood, one foot on the ground, one on the pedal of her bike, calculating.... The whales weren't headed her way.

They were headed for Decentville.... *Why there?* she asked herself. And then she realized— right past Decentville was the state capital.

Lily could only imagine what would happen if they reached the capital. They could take the whole state senate captive. They could hold the governor for ransom. Who knew what Larry had planned?

They had to be stopped.

LITTERING!

Meanwhile, Jasper was scouring the bottom of Smogascoggin Bay. His subaquatic phone rang. He cranked it quickly to get it energized, then picked up the earpiece. "Jasper Dash, Boy Technonaut," he said.

"It's Lily. I'm calling from my dad's cell phone. The whales are on their way through Decentville...I think they're heading to the state capital."

"Good golly."

There was a crackly pause. Then more softly Lily said, "My grandma lives in Decentville."

Jasper shook his head. "This is awful, Lily."

"We need to stop them."

"As soon as I can find that archvillain Larry—"

"I found out where Larry is. He's in a yacht—somewhere within sight of the Abandoned Warehouse."

"I read you," said Jasper. "I'm on it."

"Good luck!" said Lily.

"Lily," said Jasper, "don't worry about your grandma. We're prepared."

Lily didn't answer.

"Lily?"

"I've got to go," said Lily.

"Good-bye," said Jasper, "and good luck."

"You, too."

Jasper turned off the aquaphone and peered out the portholes.

Several boats hung in the water over Jasper's head. He inspected each boat for signs of anything suspicious. Nothing. He puttered farther and farther out into the bay. He put up his periscope and pulled it back down. He consulted sea charts.

This went on for some time. Jasper didn't see anything unusual. Some littering, but no real evildoing. Then, out near the islands, he came to a halt.

"Well I'll be a sandpiper's uncle," muttered Jasper. "I think I've found it." He had discovered a boat that not only had huge satellite dishes—it also had a sliding screen door underwater, very unusual on a yacht. "I'll bet that's where Larry swims out of when he wants to eat plankton."

Jasper peeked above the water with his periscope. On the deck of the yacht, guards with guns walked back and forth. Too dangerous to approach from that direction. He would have to approach from below, through the screen door.

He let the Zephyr drift to the bottom. Then he pulled on the diving bubble-suit he called the Marvelous Non-Osmotic Hypo-Allergenic Oxysphere.

He was ready to board.

LASERS ON THE PAVEMENT!

After Lily got off the phone with Jasper, she called Katie. "The whales are headed toward Decentville...where my grandmother lives... and from there, I bet they're marching to the state capital!"

"Where are you?" asked Katie.

"I'm on Highway 241, a mile or so away from the bay."

"Okay. Should we meet at the Aero-Bistro for the next stage of the plan?"

"Sure thing. But quick!"

"I'll see you there!" Katie said, and hung up.

Just as she pressed the OFF button, Katie thought she heard something loud on the other end of the line. But there was no time to lose.

She ran out to the garage and pulled on her Rollerblades. She tapped and slithered down the driveway—then set off, elbows pumping, in the direction of the Aero-Bistro.

She passed abandoned school buses and mail trucks that sat by the edge of the road. Some of the whales had walked through the neighborhood, and their massive stilt prints had torn craters into the pavement.

Cars were smashed in the middle of the street. Katie shot up onto the sidewalk to avoid them. She was whizzing along at a good speed ... when suddenly she got the feeling that something was watching her.

Keeping half an eye on the line of driveways in front of her, she looked up.

A coy whale was spying on her from behind a small shingled ranch-style garage.

She zipped past him—but saw him heave himself up to his full height.

He clomped one giant metallic foot down on the garage and began barreling toward her.

Katie's Rollerblades clattered on the road. She jumped over gratings. Her arms flew as she hurled herself forward as quickly as possible. She could hear the earth tremble as the whale pounded in hot pursuit.

He was one house away from her, kicking through a hedge.

She gasped in fear—and the lasers blasted at the pavement right in front of her.

Another blast—just to her right.

Now her left!

No time to lose, she thought.

She grabbed onto the pole of a street sign—swung around the corner—

and now was flying down a side street . . .

Made it!

Only to see that every house there was on fire.

And the whale rumbled along behind her, forcing her toward the flames.

INTERPRETATION!

Things weren't going any better for Lily. The noise on the cell phone when Katie had hung up was another platoon of whales. Lily was perched on her bicycle seat, leg extended to steady herself while she talked.

Now she heard the terrifying thrashing and crack of trees torn from their roots. The forest floor sent up little clouds of dust as each massive footfall shook the ground.

She set off, pedaling as fast as she could. She could hear the stamping of the whales not too far behind her. She went up and down paths, through little clearings. She bobbed on past the interpretive signs for the town arboretum without even reading them.

It's too bad, because there were a lot of interesting facts on those signs, if only Lily had taken a few minutes to stop and pay attention. For example, the Red (or Norway) Pine can grow up to a hundred feet tall, and can be recognized not only by the hue of its bark but also by its needles, which grow in clusters of two. The pitch of the White Pine, in olden days, was used to treat rheumatism, scurvy, and gleet. This unassuming hole was once the entrance to a fox den; it is now abandoned. If you examine the forest floor to your left, you may see a massive smoking crater; this is the spoor of the *Balaena mysticetus,* or bowhead whale. Not often seen in temperate forests, the bowhead whale and related whales, such as the Northern Right Whale (*Eubalaena glacialis*), come ashore only rarely, when remote controlled for the purposes of world domination and to eat plankton out of the treetops. Quite docile in their native element, they are singularly aggressive when on land and can only be stopped by—

But who has time to read the signs? Lily cycled on. She hurtled through groves and clearings.

A giant whale foot smashed down right beside her. She hit a rock, skidded, and wobbled. Branches flew through the air.

She threw her bike down. The whale towered above her. It had not seen her. It lifted its long legs and paced forward.

Lily staggered on the ground and crouched behind an outcropping of rock. The whales were in a line, towering above the woods. Their eyes flashed. She crowded herself backward into the curve of the outcropping. She pulled her arms and legs as close to her as she could.

The dazzle from the sun on the whales' stilts swooped across the forest floor. Lily curled up small and held her breath.

The whales walked on, following the path of destruction left by their brethren.

The crunching of tree trunks faded into the distance.

Lily stood up. The yellow of torn trees lay splintered around her.

Carefully, she picked up her bike. She looked from side to side, then climbed back on the seat and started off again. She rolled down a hillside. She wasn't far from the Aero-Bistro—fine dining in a luxurious, stratospheric atmosphere. She picked up her pace, pedaling furiously. She shot up embankments and whizzed around corners.

Which brings us back to Katie, who had just turned around a corner, only to be confronted by a street entirely filled with burning houses.

SKATE BETWEEN FLAMES!

On the street in front of Katie, houses were ablaze in a line. Black smoke churned into the sky. On either side of the road, flames slapped at the hedges.

The whale was gaining on her.

She could not go back.

She did the only thing she could: She skated even faster toward the burning block. The heat was unbearable. Everything was weirdly lit by the flames. She was getting closer to the houses.

The whale raised one leg high to stomp on her. She felt the whistle of air as its iron and titanium foot fell right behind her. The street rocked, and Katie almost lost her balance.

She knocked her skate on the road and sped up.

The whale raised his foot again—

And Katie shot between the burning shrubs, her arms outstretched for balance.

The flames licked toward her fingertips, but she was not singed.

The whale, on the other hand, could go no further. She heard him bellow as the heat scalded him, heard him cough as the smoke pouring upward into the sky engulfed him.

She grabbed another street sign and swiveled again. She was on another block now—a non-burning block.

She looked quickly behind her. Over the roofs of the houses, through the smoke, she could see the whale tottering and gagging.

I hope Lily's plan works, thought Katie.

She rattled across some train tracks.

Soon, the Aero-Bistro hung before her, sparkling in the morning light. She sped toward it down a hill. Rocks and trees blurred past her. Then Katie saw Lily.

She rolled toward the Aero-Bistro from one direction, Lily from the other.

Katie gave her friend a high five as they met, which was a good thing, since Lily just managed to grab Katie's wrist before she skated off the edge of the gorge.

They ran for the robot-operated Sky Dinghy that would take them up on deck.

There was no time to lose.

BATTLE AT SEA!

Meanwhile, Jasper had got his undersea equipment together and had drifted up to the sliding screen door in the bottom of Larry's yacht.

Jasper's undersea gear consisted of a striped bathing costume, a sea captain's hat, a wicked-looking harpoon gun, and the Oxysphere, a giant wobbly bubble-suit that encased him entirely. He had to really warp the Oxysphere to get it through the yacht's doorway. Once he fit it through, he bobbed up above the level of the water.

Jasper emerged in a pool inside the yacht. Carefully he climbed out of the pool. Falling back in a few times. Because it is not easy to climb when encased in a giant wobbly bubble. It really isn't.

Here, for example, is British adventurer Lesley Gorbuckle-Smythe in the third volume of his autobiography, *Between a Rock and Hard Place: The Travels, Memoirs, and Derring-do of Lesley Gorbuckle-Smythe*: "Beastly tiring, it was, ascending Mount Everest. After the third day the Sherpa who was leading me took me aside. He suggested that perhaps I should continue the ascent without the ten-foot-wide latex bubble. Well, I told the little blighter that an Englishman's latex bubble was his castle, his kingdom, his motte and his bailey, and that..." etc., etc., etc.

The above quotation gave Jasper enough time to get out of the water finally and stand beside the pool. He was crouched and ready for anything. He brandished his harpoon gun. He crept to the door and cranked it open.

There were bunks, with sleeping guards on them, lining the walls. Jasper rolled through very quietly. There was only a very little shrieking, squealing noise as the Marvelous Non-Osmotic

Hypo-Allergenic Oxysphere squeezed between the bunks.

Jasper opened the next door and prepared to roll through.

It was a control room. Larry sat there at a big computer console, pushing buttons. Giant screens showed a whale's-eye-view of the countryside.

Perfect.

Jasper declared bravely, "The game is up, you cad! Resist, and you'll find a harpoon buried deep in your blubbery parts!"

Larry turned to face him. Larry no longer had on the grain sack. His head was blue and bumpy, with small mammalian eyes and a sneering mouth full of baleen. It was, in other words, a face that looked like

a mixture of seafood and unsuccessful rhinoplasty.

rhinoplasty [ry-no-plast-y] *n* cosmetic surgery performed on the nose. Example: "My irritable whale cousin slammed the door in my face, almost performing an impromptu *rhinoplasty.*"

"Is that so, kid?" asked Larry. "Is that really so?"

"Yes, sir," said Jasper. He raised his harpoon within his plastic bubble. "I will not hesitate to use my—"

And then he felt the guns sticking into his back, pressing against the Oxysphere. The guards had woken up.

On the screens the whales were within sight of Decentville.

DECENTVILLE IN DANGER!

Meanwhile, on land, the whales were within sight of Decentville.

Already on the streets of that little town, there was panic. People running out of the five-and-dime could see whales tottering toward them on the horizon. Farmhouses were on fire. Laser-beam eyes flashed.

Explosions rocked Decentville.

Cars were stopped in the middle of roads so people could run into discount clothing stores. Smoke was pouring out of the gas station. A pop machine had ruptured; dogs licked up Dr Pepper from the pavement.

And somewhere in all of that chaos, Lily's grandmother lived.

Lily and Katie saw all this from the Aero-Bistro. The androids had turned on the propellers, and the airship was headed to meet the whales. Meanwhile, Katie and Lily were putting their plan into action. They ran around on the dining deck, setting up phonograph record players, aiming the huge sound bells toward the whales.

Clouds drifted under the Aero-Bistro. It puttered toward the evil pod.

The whales were readying for the kill.

The android waiters dolefully told customers, "This is not happy hour."

CHEW VIGOROUSLY!

Lily's grandmother was just coming out of the five-and-dime with some half-price ribbon candy. It was amazing how cheap you could get ribbon candy when it was smashed.

Lily's grandma figured it didn't matter if the ribbon candy was a little broken, because you chewed it, anyway, so it was always smashed by the time it reached your gullet. She didn't understand why people made such a fuss about things that were just going to get torn up by your teeth before they got to your gullet, anyhow. For example, a piece of chicken. What was the difference between a piece of chicken on your plate looking all nice and neat as a button, and a piece of chicken on your plate that had already been chewed by your brother Nate? Not a goll-blasted thing. And if people couldn't understand that, well then—

But her train of thought was broken. There, towering over her, was the first of the whales to stomp into Decentville. It was huge. It glared down at her.

Its eyes were sparkling. The lasers were warming up.

Lily's grandmother screamed.

CAPTURED!

But let's get back to the adventures of Jasper Dash, Boy Technonaut.

As you may recall, our plucky pal was standing in the control room on Larry's yacht, encased entirely in a bubble, while guards poked their guns into his back. Jasper was beginning to wish that his bubble wasn't quite so wobbly.

It was a dire moment for our boy hero.

Just the kind of opportunity that mad scientists take to explain to their victims their plots for world domination.

Larry, thankfully, did nothing of the kind, as his plan for world domination was really pretty straightforward—have whales invade everything—and didn't exactly require a map, a lecture course, and a Boolean diagram to explain.

So the good news was that Jasper didn't have to listen to Larry drone on about how soon—soon!—the world would be his—*his, do you hear? his*—etc. The bad news was that there really was nothing to delay Larry, or to convince him that he shouldn't just shoot Jasper immediately.

Jasper's eyes were full of bravery and defiance, but in his heart he didn't see any way out, and he was counting his blessings in this life, chief among them being that he had always done what his mother had asked. He was also proud of his friendship with two of the bravest and most resourceful girls alive, Katie Mulligan and Lily Gefelty. And he was proud, finally, that each and every morning he had started the day right, with Gargletine Brand Patented Breakfast Drink, the wonderfully effective, chocolaty-good cure for what ails you.

Jasper whispered silent good-byes to those he loved.

And Larry said, "The whales have just reached Decentville. Off the kid, and let's get moving."

GREATEST HITS!

The whales were stepping over and on buildings, spreading themselves out through the town, preparing for mass destruction.

Lily's grandmother, on the ground, quivered with fear and dropped her bargain candy.

"That's my grandma!" said Lily, leaning over the railing of the Aero-Bistro.

"Concentrate, Lily!" said Katie. "We've got to put your plan into action."

Lily raised herself up. The fate of the world was in her hands.

The Aero-Bistro hovered near the whales. Along the railing was the series of phonograph record players—and by each one stood a robotic waiter.

The whales swiveled on their electronic stilt-legs and faced the airship. Their eyes glittered.

They were ready to shoot. They were ready to blast the Aero-Bistro out of the sky.

From below people screamed and tried to get out from under the restaurant's shadow.

The whale eyes burned.

Lily said, "Go!"

The waiters, in unison, dropped the needles onto the records.

"Take that!" said Katie.

The gramophone records played. In unison, with a few pops and cracks, the songs of the humpback whale filled the air. The whooping and creaking. The empty echoes through the ocean depths.

The whales hesitated. They listened.

"It's working!" said Katie. "They're distracted by their own whale song!"

But it wasn't enough.

Their eyes still sparkled.

Lily gasped. "Jasper must not have blocked the signal from Larry's radio tower yet!"

"Oh no!" cried Katie. "If music can't save us, what can?"

!!!!!!!!!!!!!!!!!!!!

The answer, my friends—and this isn't the answer Katie was expecting—was a trussed-up man named Ray.

Ray, you may remember, was a friend of Mr. Gefelty's who was dragged away from work all tied up and gagged because He Knew Too Much. He had been thrown on board Larry's yacht until he could be fed to the narwhals.

Ray, however, was not one to be thrown overboard lightly. He didn't just sit there waiting to walk the plank. No, he hopped down the corridor, ready to pick a fight without even the use of his hands.

He saw his opportunity when he passed the control room door and glimpsed some kid in a

HEIGH-HO, LADS!

THROW DOWN YOUR SCOOTERS AND COME RUNNING! IT'S TIME FOR YET ANOTHER MIND-BOGGLING ADVENTURE

— WITH —

Jasper Dash, Boy Technonaut!

Yes, boys of America! You've thrilled to the tales of Jasper fighting crime wherever it rears its ugly and unshaven head—from Tierra del Fuego to the Arctic Circle! You've shivered as he's discovered lost cities! You've cheered as he's tangled with snakes and with vampire frogs, as he's jousted with princes, slugged crooks, bartered with moon-men, and been trussed up and sold for bait by sinister gondoliers! You've dropped your jaw like a red-hot manhole cover as he flew in his marvelous inventions past startling vistas—and took you to see things like *nothing else in the world of literature!* And it's all ***completely scientific!*** Why, there's not a bit of hoopla or sass in Jasper Dash—Boy Technonaut!

If you haven't read the following titles, then by golly get up from the table and leave the screen door flapping as you rocket downtown to purchase . . .

AVAILABLE AT FINE STORES NEAR YOU!*

Jasper Dash

is a red-blooded American boy who provides a shining example of the virtues that made this nation great: honesty, pluck, courage, arm strength, courteousness to elders, cleanliness, ingenuity, friendliness, and regularity of bowel movements. And where does he come by these excellent virtues? Nowhere but in the dregs of his morning glass of...

GARGLETINE BREAKFAST DRINK

Say, Kids:

"Want to Feel All Peachy Keen?
Drink a Quart of Gargletine!"

---

*No longer available on the shelves at fine stores near you. Available now *exclusively and by special arrangement* on the shelves of old vacation rental cottages, where you can often find Jasper Dash books in the living room, as well

173

stupid bubble being held at gunpoint by Larry's goons.

And hurled himself bodily into them.

Ray came flying into the room, knocking down several goons. Jasper, reacting as quick as lightning, knocked a goon over the head with the butt of his harpoon gun while, with the other hand, he gripped another goon under his arm in a headlock.

Now if you'll pause for a moment and consider, you'll remember that Jasper was still in his bubble. This meant that the man in the headlock had bubble-bag over his head and couldn't breathe. So, he started kicking his legs and arms.

Larry advanced menacingly toward them.

---

as old *National Geographic*s, Chinese checkers, half colored-in Herbie the Love Bug activity books from 1978, used up Mad Libs, and dog-eared, boring novels for adults by Leon Uris, Colleen McCullough, and James Michener, I mean big, thick books with names like *Space* and *Novel*, you know what I mean, right on the shelf under the dead mounted alligator that Sheryl, your uncle Georgie's new girlfriend, has to keep turning toward the wall because it gives her the creeps. And all the books are dry and yellow from the sun, and all of them have wrinkly pages from the salt water, and

There was a big fight. Most of the goons were knocked out or in some kind of disarray.

That sounds sloppy. But please. Take my word for it; they were out of the picture, okay? I could describe the whole tedious fight. I could work it out numerically and mathematically, but goons—and hand-to-hand combat with goons; anything to do with goons—it all really bores me to the point of weeping. Their equipment, their martial arts training, their love of dried flowers, their fondness for sports bars...I am not goon friendly. *Bing, bang, biff.* Clocked on the jaw; hip check; knee to the nose; leap out of the way so two of them run into each other; swing; *pow;* knuckle sandwich. Let's just assume that they're all knocked out.

------

when you flip through them, sand falls out as if it was index cards marking the place of former summers; and your little brother Dooky finds some half-melted army men on the shelf and goes out to the sandpit to play with them, which is good, because he was completely getting on your nerves in the car, what with his dumb elephant joke that he told about twenty thousand times; but after him spending like an hour out there, you'll be ready to talk to him again, especially if the two of you can convince your mom to let you go out to dinner at this place that serves spicy fries. And the really

Larry advanced menacingly toward Ray and Jasper.

Ray hurled himself again, this time right at Larry.

Larry raised one rubbery blue fist and knocked him backward. Ray teetered and slumped, still tied up like a beach umbrella in February. It was up to Jasper.

Jasper raised his harpoon gun. Larry spun and kicked. His heel whopped the edge of the bubble, knocked the harpoon gun askew just as the harpoon was fired. The harpoon shot through the bubble and clanged uselessly against the ceiling.

---

good thing about Uncle Georgie always having new girlfriends is that the new girlfriends are always really, really nice to you because they're trying to impress Uncle Georgie, before they realize that he's nice but kind of a wiener and has a big gambling problem; and you think Sheryl is probably the best girlfriend that he's had in a long time, because at least she can do card tricks, so on the beach, you sit next to her on your blanket, and you're reading the adventures of Jasper Dash and you're wondering who originally read them, years ago, who were the faceless kids, now grandmas or now dead, who lay like you on the beach and read them back when your parents

Larry laughed—for
about a nanosecond.
And then he saw what
was happening:

Jasper's pierced bubble was deflating with
Jasper in it—shooting around the room like a
punctured balloon—making a disastrous sput-
tering noise as Jasper ricocheted off the walls—
banged into light fixtures—slammed into computer panels.

Jasper Dash, Boy Technonaut, was interfer-
ing with the whale mind-control, using only his
elbows, face, and midriff.

Now that's a hero for you.

And in Smogascoggin Bay, the radio tower
stopped sending out its wicked signals.

---

weren't even born yet, and their names are written in pencil on the first
page—"This book belongs to Caroline Botts"; "Hank Botts read it, too"—
but the people who own the cottage you're renting are called Martelli. Your
older sister Gina refused to put on suntan lotion for some reason, so now
her skin is all purple and green, and a lot of the local boys have come over
to admire it, and they're going, "Whoa! Cool!" and she smiles at them, with
a kind of crackling sound as the skin on her face moves. And your mom
and Uncle Georgie are playing Frisbee on the beach, calling to each other,
and Sheryl is lying there next to you, studying for some graduate school

And in Decentville, the whales paused and listened to the whale song Lily played on the phonographs.

They heard their brethren from the sea. Their minds suddenly felt clearer.

From the phonographs came the lonely cries of whales on ancient voyages, barnacled with age. They heard songs that told of warmer climes, where the sun dapples your back when you sound with your calf in the afternoons; tales of the mysterious North, where ice floes like castles drop their battlements into the chilly sea. They heard of their race's heroes, and of

exam, wearing big sunglasses; and Gina has just gotten sand in her sand-wich and is complaining about it to everyone, because she says it *clings* to the swiss cheese, like *clings*, you know? and everyone is going, "Just brush it off," and she says she can't, because her hands are sandy, and Dooky says, "What are you complaining about? Sand...Sand-*wich*. Sand...Sand-*wich*," which actually is pretty funny, because it makes Gina even angrier, and she goes, "Mom! Tell him to stop being a jerk!" And the top of your head gets warm as you read on about Jasper's adventures in the cloud caves, and you don't even notice the green flies buzzing around you anymore, their travels to frigid deeps. They heard of the slumberous beauty of tides, the seductive murmur of kelp.

And the whales wanted to go home.

Sheepishly they looked at one another.

Without mind-control they couldn't remember what they were doing on land at all.

So they started to walk back to the shore, trying to pretend that nothing had happened.

In the town they left behind, there was cheering.

---

and you've spent nights having clambakes down by the ocean, and you had a lobster for the first time, and Gina was allergic, and she got hives and piles, so she looked like she was leopard skin, a leopard-skin Gina, and Sheryl was really good with her and helped her apply ointment, and Dooky kept going, "*Oink*ment, more like it"; and you brush flies away from your hair, and your uncle, who is sitting next to you, trying to hitch a flying kite to his leg, sees you, and somehow overcome, your uncle Georgie smiles— and he says to you, "I hope you will always feel this kind of joy"; and motorboats go by out in the salt marsh, and they startle egrets so they fly up toward the empty, cloudless sky.

BRINE AND WHINE

Larry watched the screens in despair. "My army...my army!"

Jasper picked himself up from the floor, struggling a bit with the deflated Oxysphere around him. "I'm afraid they're gone, sir. Gone back to the sea, where they belong."

One after another, the whales tumbled into the water, their stilts lying desolate, like hydraulic pickup sticks, on the shore.

"It's all ruined!" Larry growled.

By this point Ray had freed himself from the ropes and picked up one of the guns from the floor. Larry strode right past him, knocking his hand aside. Larry turned at the door. He growled, "I'm going to swim away, through my yacht's screen door. But mark my word, Boy Technonaut—I'll be back. You'll see me again! Someday I'll be back, and more fearsome than ever!"

Jasper looked at him, tight lipped. "No, sir, I'm afraid not." He shook his head solemnly.

"No?"

"No," Jasper said, very gently and consolingly. "In three years I'll run into you, and you'll be working full-time at an industrial carpet-cleaning service."

Larry's head drooped. He said sadly, "The one on Ethan Boulevard?"

"No," said Jasper, "a little farther south, on the corner of Twelfth and Harrison. You'll be writing your memoirs at night."

Larry nodded. "They'll be too long and boring for publication, won't they?"

Jasper felt he shouldn't answer this. He put his hand, still webbed with bubble, on Larry's shoulder. "You gave it your best go, sir. That's all any of us can do."

"Thank you," said Larry. "I'll see you some other time."

"Remember, evil never pays."

"Okay," said Larry. "Thanks for...you know, the tip and all." He shuffled off to an unforgiving future.

Meanwhile, Jasper Dash gasped for breath, trying to find the way out of his Marvelous Non-Osmotic Hypo-Allergenic Oxysphere.

THREE FOR ONE

A week later a very triumphant little party was gathered in the Aero-Bistro, floating over the sea. Of course, Lily, Jasper, and Katie were there. They were joined by their parents and the governor of the state, who was congratulating Lily on her brilliant scheme to foil Larry's invasion.

"Lily, it's quite a feat. You really have shown the people of this state what one girl can do," the governor said. "Just one girl, some androids, a flying restaurant, twenty vintage Victrola phonograph players, a small submarine, and a boy in a plastic bubble."

Katie said, "She's the one who first noticed that there was something fishy about the Abandoned Warehouse."

Jasper said, "And she's the one who figured out what Larry's plan was."

Katie said, "And she's the one who figured out how we could remind the whales of what they were missing underwater. She figured it out by listening to her grandmother."

The governor nodded. "I hate to think what would have happened if you hadn't stepped in, Lily. If those whales had made it to the state capital...I see an awful picture in my head: whales in the state legislature, wearing white wigs... making lots of laws...where schoolkids had to eat plankton...It makes me proud to be a non-whale elected official of this great state." He smiled for the cameras.

Several of Katie's writers from Harcourt were at the next table. "Lily," said one, "when you first saw Barry the fish-man, did your eyes 'stick out' in horror?"

The second writer lit a cigarette. "When you thought of your plan, I assume you said, 'It's so crazy...it *just might work.*' I'm writing that down: ... *so crazy ... it ... just ... might ...*"

"Lily, do you have any superpowers you haven't told us about?"

"Here. Bend my keys with your mind."

Lily took a step backward.

"Do you ever wear a cape and a bodysuit?"

"A crash helmet?"

"You really need a pet rat named Nimrod. He's a scoundrel, but he'll worm his way into your heart."

"Be quiet!" yelled Katie.

The three men stopped their scribbling and typing.

"All this attention is frazzling her," said Katie.

Lily looked at her own knees.

For a second, the three writers looked ashamed.

Then one of them said, "Mr. Dash, when you fought off the killer bees, did you—"

Katie grabbed her friends' arms and pointed.

She, Lily, and Jasper pulled away from all the people who wanted to hear their story, and they stepped over to the railing to watch the sun set over the sea. Around them the potted ferns waved and the seagulls cried. The clouds turned a rich, rumbling kind of red as the sun disappeared. The sky stretched peach above their heads. The wind blew at them.

Katie said, "Well, Lily—are you proud?"

Lily didn't say anything. She just smiled and nodded.

Jasper looked at her. He said shyly, "Why—Lily—with your hair blown back like that—you're beautiful."

Lily quickly covered her eyes with her bangs.

Katie shook her head. "Walking whales," she said. "Is there a single weird thing that doesn't happen to us?"

"Could have been worse, fellows," said Jasper. "It could have been evil, flying kelp. Or giant man-eating sea anemones."

Katie shrugged. "With fiends like these, who needs anemones?"

She grinned and spread her hands.

"Katie," said Jasper, "we could laugh, but that would be like lying to a friend."

He turned to look at the clouds. Katie punched him lightly on the arm. Jasper just whistled a tune and kept looking at the clouds. Katie leaned her elbows on the railing next to him. Jasper kicked Katie in the shin, in a polite, gentlemanly kind of way. Katie, admiring the way the water reflected the light, put her pinkie in Jasper's ear. Jasper took his elbow and—

"Break it up," said Lily, "or I'm throwing my Jell-O at both of you."

Along the shore, the forest and the gorge turned red with sunset. For a long time, they stood by the railing and talked about things that mattered to them. There are times when friendship feels like running down a hill together as fast as you can, jumping over things, spinning around, and you don't care where you're going, and you don't care where you've come from, because all that matters is speed, and the hands holding your hands. That's how it felt to Katie, Jasper, and Lily: Though the night was falling, it was as if they could still feel the sun on their faces, and they stood together talking until the sky turned to black, the party balloons sagged, and the androids came to take them home.

A Guide for Reading and Thinking

Questions for further study

We hope that you have enjoyed *Whales on Stilts*. Many readers may be coming across this book for the first time in a classroom setting or in a structured reading group; for them we have endeavored to provide questions to aid in a thoughtful and insightful conversation about the themes, characters, and real-world story that the author, M. T. Anderson, has woven into the rich tapestry that is this book. The editors at Harcourt have employed child-learning specialist Ann Mowbray Dixon-Clarke to come up with a series of talking-points that will enrich, enliven, and enlighten.

When everyone in your group is seated comfortably, the designated moderator should begin by asking the following questions:

1. Who chose this book?

2. Can I hit him/her in the stomach?

3. Which character is your favorite character?

4. Out of all the page numbers in the book, which one is your favorite? Discuss.

5. What's that out the window?

6. If you could legally drive any whale at all, would you drive a baleen whale (Suborder Mysticeti) or a toothed whale (Suborder Odontoceti)? (Please show your work.)

7. In the scene with the giant starfish, who should have picked up the powdered sugar?
    a. Katie
    b. Jasper
    c. Maeve
    d. Whoever spilled it, thank you very much
    e. Nimrod, the debonair pet rat. What antics!

8. Which whale book with a character named Lily and another one named Jasper is your favorite?

9. Oh, really?

10. Lily notices many strange things around the streets of Pelt. What strange things do you notice around your town?

11. Should you report something like that to the police?

12. Jasper Dash owns a pair of electric pants. If you could electrify any article of your best friend's clothing, which would it be, and how many volts?

13. What do you think the theme of this work is? Please hum it in its entirety.

14. When you are reading this book and you begin to weep, is it because of:
    a. the plight of Pelt
    b. the terror of whales
    c. too many fictional helmets
    d. you are reading this book
    e. Ann Mowbray Dixon-Clarke

15. Anchovies: Why?

16. In one scene, Jasper Dash wears a futuristic photocopier-repair outfit. If you were walking down the street and one of your friends came up in a futuristic outfit, for example some futuristic shorts or maybe a futuristic swim cap—on a bright, sunny day, let's say, and the swim cap was green and sparkly, and this friend comes up, and you haven't seen her for three days because you've had a lot of work to do

around the yard because your parents hate saplings, and you've been burying your head in *The Chronicles of Chowder #7: The Saw That Cut Time,* and haven't come to the phone ever when your friend called, and now you see that your friend is wearing this outfit, and across the street there are three guys who you know a little bit from 4-H, would . . . um . . . I forget the question. Could I borrow some gum?

17. Larry: Would anyone call him cuddly?

ESSAY QUESTIONS

by Ann Mowbray Dixon-Clarke

1.   How are Katie, Jasper, and Lily different? Why do you think they are friends? Do you have any friends who are very different from you? What are they like? Why don't you think that Ann Mowbray Dixon-Clarke has any friends? She bought a big grill for her backyard, hoping that people would come to cook their ribs. She has that great dress with the twisty things on the arms. Do you think she's different? Is she *distinctively* different, i.e., *with a certain flair*?

2.   Why do the whales decide to go home? What do they miss about their home? If you are in a classroom or a reading group, do you wish you were at home right now? Do you wish you were at Ann Mowbray Dixon-Clarke's home, where there are ribs a-plenty? Maybe you could bring your class and some coleslaw.

3.   Larry is a bad person in most of this book. Do you think he could become a good person? What would make the difference in Larry's life?

Maybe he needs the love and attention of a very special lady, who can help him choose his suits and grain sacks, someone who can spray his flukes, someone who could help him channel those destructive energies into the building of birdhouses and the cooking of ribs in her darling backyard. Who might that person be? Have you read about anyone recently who might be the perfect person for a handsome, rubbery, concealed overachiever like Larry?

4. Many old-time novels end with a marriage. *Whales on Stilts* does not. It ends with robots. I like it when books end with some hand-holding, flowers, and distant bees. If you could choose a place for a wedding to end this novel, would you choose the Chapel in the Dozing Glen or the Wee Kirk in the Heather? How would you dress the bridesmaids? Should the groomsmen wear tuxedos? (Remember: They are whales.)

by Ann Mowbray Dixon-Clarke

Ann Mowbray Dixon-Clarke: *What gave you the idea for this book?*

M. T. Anderson: Indigestion.

A. M. D.-C.: *What had you eaten?*

M. T. A.: I live alone and cook for myself. So, I think it was gravel. Gravel's not so bad if you own a Fry-o-Lator.

A. M. D.-C.: *Okay, you know what's good? Ribs and coleslaw.*

M. T. A.: Thanks. I'll keep that in mind.

A. M. D.-C.: *What were your favorite books when you were a kid?*

M. T. A.: Of course, I loved all of the Jasper Dash books, and they were one of my main inspirations for writing *Whales on Stilts.* On long Saturday afternoons, I would turn off the television when

the cartoons were over and go to the local library.
I'd trot down the stairs to the basement, where
they kept all of the old books that hadn't made it
onto the electronic database. I would sit there and
read a Jasper Dash adventure, and suddenly I
would feel myself part of this community of
readers, kids from the fifties with buzz-cut hair
and kids from the seventies with necklaces
made of shells, all of us in awe before the same
wondrous stories, all of us meeting in the space
of the imagination.

A. M. D.-C.: *It sounds like you were kind of lonely
as a kid. Is that true?*

M. T. A.: Not really. I had my friends and my
books, and we made up worlds together.

A. M. D.-C.: *If you were lonely, would you have
liked to have been invited to a wedding with some
ribs and slaw? Between a child-learning specialist
with a certain flair and a whale-human hybrid? Did
you ever think of* that *on a Saturday afternoon,
when you were lying on the rug, a book open in
front of you, the sun falling through the basement
window, the savor of library paste and uncertain*

patrons in the air? Did you think that you might want to be at a whale-human hybrid wedding with a garden nook and a bagpiper playing Pachelbel's Canon and Gigue, *the smell of hollyhocks and ham hocks mingling by the grill, and Jasper and Lily and Katie sitting on folding chairs, all looking at each other like they'd be kind of relieved to be somewhere else? And then, suddenly, coming down the aisle, is the most handsome whale-human hybrid you've ever seen, the ruffles on his shirt as blue as the balmy Caribbean, free now to show his face to a world that never loved him and the woman who does, and who always shall, with all her soul? Did you imagine the laughter afterward on the porch, the kiss beneath the ivied bower—the rapturous kiss, with the tang of baleen, the scent of foreign seas?*

Did you, author? Did you foresee this, the dancing till dawn? Did you?

Did you?

Great scott, chums!
Turn the page for a peek at the next
thrilling tale by M. T. Anderson:

THE CLUE OF THE
LINOLEUM LEDERHOSEN

Jasper, Lily, and Katie walked down a sweeping staircase into the lobby of the Moose Tongue Lodge and Resort.

The lobby was cavernous. On the walls were old moose-hide snowshoes and wooden skis. There was a birch-bark canoe hanging above the front desk. A row of mounted animal heads hung high on the wall. People were bustling everywhere. Porters were taking bags; bellhops in pillbox hats were squeaking, "Yes, ma'am!" and bowing; there were lots of big men in raccoon-skin coats and pinstripe suits smoking cigars and pointing at portraits on the walls. The portraits were of famous men and their horses and hounds. One was of a sportfisherman with his trained eel, Loopy. Another man in a portrait had a falcon on his gloved arm.

Jasper walked right up to the front desk.

"Hello," he said. "We're Jasper Dash, Lily Gefelty, and Katie Mulligan. We've just taken those rooms in that new tower addition, rooms 23A–E, off the bathroom of 46B."

"Oh, Mr. . . . Mr. Dash? *The* Jasper Dash? Boy Technonaut?"

Jasper looked humbly at the inkwell. "Yes. Yes, that's me, sir."

"It's great to meet you!" said the man at the desk. "We just cleared a whole bunch of your books out of the lounge library! Burned a whole stack of them!"

"Ah," said Jasper, looking at his toes.

"Hey, you aren't the only child hero at the hotel this weekend. We got the Cutesy Dell Twins, the Manley Boys, and those adorable mystery-solving Hooper Quints! You know, the Quintuplets!"

Jasper explained to the man at the desk, "We

have come to redeem our coupon for a free dinner."

"A free dinner?" said Katie.

"I always try to be frugal when I travel," said Jasper, "as well as clean and well mannered." He pulled out a photocopied coupon for a free dinner. "I received this last week."

The man at the desk looked at it. "Eh, nah," he said. "No. Nope." He handed it back. "Not real."

"What do you mean by 'not real'?" asked Jasper.

"This isn't from us."

"Then who is it from?"

"Why would I know?" asked the man at the desk.

Katie pressed, "Who would send us a fake coupon to your restaurant this weekend?"

"That's not something I know," said the man at the desk. "But whoever they are, they sent out a bunch of them. Like to the Cutesy Dell Twins." He pointed over Jasper's head.

There was a commotion near the front door. A man ran in screaming.

"They've been kidnapped!" he yelled. "They're gone!"

"Who?" yelled someone convenient.

"The Hooper Quints! All five of them! They're all gone! Someone took them!"